'What the devil is going on?' he snapped.

'I'm. . .s-sorry,' stammered Pippa. 'The bag burst.' Helplessly she indicated her possessions strewn around the hall and stairs.

'Don't you realise there are people in this house on night duty who are trying to sleep?' he went on, apparently disregarding her rather feeble explanation. 'And there are some of us who are trying to work,' he added angrily. 'Who are you, anyway?'

Pippa took a deep breath. 'I've just moved in to number four,' she said firmly.

With a scathing glance at her scattered possessions, he spread his hands in a gesture of contempt. 'God help us!'

Laura MacDonald lives on the Isle of Wight. She is married and has a grown-up family. She has enjoyed writing fiction since she was a child, but for several years she has worked for members of the medical profession both in pharmacy and in general practice. Her daughter is a nurse and has also helped with the research for Laura's Medical Romances.

Previous Titles

ALWAYS ON MY MIND
AN UNEXPECTED AFFAIR
ISLAND PARTNER

LOVE CHANGES EVERYTHING

BY

LAURA MacDONALD

MILLS & BOON LIMITED
ETON HOUSE   18–24 PARADISE ROAD
RICHMOND   SURREY   TW9 1SR

*First published in Great Britain 1991
by Mills & Boon Limited*

© Laura MacDonald 1991

*Australian copyright 1991
Philippine copyright 1991
This edition 1991*

ISBN 0 263 77498 8

*Set in 10½ on 12 pt Linotron Palatino
03-9112-49325
Typeset in Great Britain by Centracet, Cambridge
Made and printed in Great Britain*

CHAPTER ONE

'However did you accumulate all this junk in just two years, Pippa?' Claire French groaned as she began unloading boxfuls of books and records from the back seat of the Citroën 2CV.

'I didn't; most of it I brought with me from home.' Philippa Ward grinned, and, pausing for a moment, she stared across the forecourt at the large house. 'I need my things around me—it stops me from getting too homesick.'

Claire grunted as she heaved a black plastic sack out on to the gravel. 'I can't imagine where you ever found room for it all at the nurses' home— those rooms are so small.'

'Oh, I packed it all in somehow,' replied Pippa, airily pushing back stray tendrils of her long dark hair. 'But this will be so much better. Two years in a nurses' home is enough for anyone.' As she spoke she glanced up at the red-brick, half-timbered house with its black ornamental gables and fresh white paintwork. 'I couldn't believe my luck when I heard about this flat,' she added as she hauled two large suitcases from the boot of her car.

'I must agree it looks better than the average hospital accommodation,' admitted Claire. 'In fact it looks a darn sight better than where I'm living. You'd better let me know if another one comes vacant.'

It was a cold December morning, but both girls, dressed warmly in thick sweaters and jeans, seemed oblivious to the chill in the air as they carried Pippa's belongings into the porchway of Maple House. The heavy oak front door had stained-glass panels on either side and on the wall to the left was a column of doorbells with little plastic sections indicating the names of the occupants of the eight flats within the house.

'That's me—number four.' Pippa pointed excitedly to the one empty section, then fumbled in her pocket for the set of keys she had been given the day before. While Claire waited patiently behind her she fitted one of the keys into the Yale lock and the door swung open.

The house was quiet except for the faint sound of a radio being played softly in one of the ground-floor flats and the distant hum of a vacuum-cleaner. The hallway with its black and white tiled floor was lined with several large pieces of oak furniture. The staircase was covered with red vinyl that had obviously seen better days, but in spite of an air of almost genteel shabbiness the place was clean.

'Whereabouts is your flat?' asked Claire, looking hopefully round the hall.

'Upstairs,' replied Pippa cheerfully.

'How did I know you were going to say that?' Claire groaned again, then picked up the boxes that she'd set down on the tiled floor.

'Well, it could be worse. At least I'm on the first floor and not the second.'

Claire followed Pippa up the stairs, and on the first floor landing they stopped at the doorway marked with a large number four, and, while Pippa once again sorted out her keys, Claire sniffed the air. 'What's that nice smell?' she asked.

Pippa paused with the key in the lock and lifted her head. 'I'm not sure—some sort of polish or air-freshener, I suppose. . . I know! It's. . .it's honeysuckle.'

'Yes, I think you're right,' agreed Claire. 'Pippa,' she added urgently, and as her friend turned anxiously, before pushing open the flat door, she asked, 'Why are we whispering?'

Pippa stared solemnly at Claire's tiny pointed face beneath a wispy blonde fringe, then suddenly she grinned. 'I don't know.'

Both girls dissolved into fits of giggles and fell into the flat, collapsing in a heap of cases, boxes and plastic bags in the centre of the floor.

After they'd sorted themselves out Claire began to wander round the flat. The main living area was really a large bedsit with a sofa that converted to a bed at night. A tiny kitchenette was partitioned off at one end of the room and at the other a shower unit.

'This is super,' said Claire enviously. 'I'm still sharing with Tracey and Mai-lee, and I'm fed up with it. At least here you'll be able to do what you like, when you like.'

Pippa nodded. 'Exactly!' She flung herself down on the sofa with a sigh of satisfaction and looked around at the high-ceilinged room emulsioned in a soft duck-egg blue. The flat was basically but adequately furnished, and she knew that in a short space of time, when she had all her precious bits and pieces in place, she could transform it to feel

like home. 'It'll be wonderful to have the freedom
to do as I please,' she went on. 'If I want to throw
a party I can, and if I want to be quiet I can. But
talking of quiet,' she frowned, 'it's a bit too quiet
around here.' Then, catching sight of her radio on
the top of one of the boxes Claire had carried up,
she reached forward and picked it up. It was
already tuned to Radio One, and as she flicked the
switch, the strains of her current favourite chart-
topper filled the room.

She grinned at Claire. 'That's better,' she said.
'Sounds like home now.'

'I suppose we'd better get the rest of your things
in,' said Claire with an exaggerated sigh.

'No, I'll tell you what, we'll have a cup of tea
first,' said Pippa. 'Look, there are some mugs over
there in that cupboard, but I've got my own kettle.
Now where did I put it?' She looked round. 'Oh, I
remember, it's in that other black bag in the car.
I'll just nip down and get it.'

Leaving the flat door open so that she could still
hear the music, Pippa ran lightly down the stairs
and out to the car. There was still one very large
black plastic bag in the boot; it was almost filled
with her collection of fluffy animals, but at the top
she had put her few saucepans and her kettle.

She picked up the bag, then hesitated, wondering if she could manage to carry anything else,
then from the back seat she pulled out a pile of her
clothes still on their hangers. With the clothes over
one arm and dragging the black bag behind her
she went back into the house and slowly began to
climb the stairs.

She had nearly reached the top when the bag,

strained to its limits, suddenly burst. The soft toys cascaded harmlessly down the stairs and bounced over the banisters, but the kettle, her three saucepans and the frying-pan clattered and banged down the entire staircase on to the tiled floor of the hall below. Pippa watched helplessly as the din seemed to go on for ever, until the last saucepan lid finally spun to a halt and with a final clatter came to rest by the front door.

In the comparative silence in the few seconds that followed even the music from the radio seemed distant. Then Claire's anxious face appeared over the banisters at the same moment as another door on the landing was flung open and a man appeared. Claire had a fleeting impression of a tall slim figure, dark hair that flopped over his forehead and cool grey eyes behind horn-rimmed glasses. His expression, however, as he leaned on the banisters and looked down at her, was one of exasperation.

'What the devil is going on?' he snapped.

'I'm. . .s-sorry,' stammered Pippa. 'The bag burst.' Helplessly she indicated her possessions strewn around the hall and stairs.

'Don't you realise there are people in this house on night duty who are trying to sleep?' he went on, apparently disregarding her rather feeble explanation. 'And there are some of us who are trying to work,' he added angrily.

Pippa swallowed and glanced beyond him to an open doorway that revealed a glimpse of a room with book-lined shelves and the corner of a desk. She shrugged apologetically. 'I've said I'm sorry. . .it wasn't my fault. . .the bag——'

'Yes, I know, so it wasn't your fault, but what about that racket?' He jerked his thumb over his shoulder towards her flat where the sound of Dire Straits could be heard blaring out from her radio. 'I suppose that isn't your fault either?' There was definite sarcasm in his tone now, and Pippa felt herself stiffen. She had been more than prepared to be apologetic if she had caused a nuisance, but suddenly she felt resentful of his rudeness.

She glanced up the stairs again and saw that Claire had disappeared, then almost immediately the radio was switched off. The man was still watching her, and she noticed he was dressed in a white open-necked shirt and dark cord trousers. She judged him to be somewhere in his thirties.

'Who are you, anyway?' She jumped as he spoke sharply again. 'What are you doing here? I haven't seen you before.' His frown had deepened as he glared at her over the top of his glasses, taking in every detail of her dress, her long dark hair that tumbled over her shoulders and her large brown eyes.

She took a deep breath. 'I've just moved in to number four,' she said firmly.

With another scathing glance at her scattered possessions, the fluffy pandas, owls and other animals and the kitchen utensils, he spread his hands in a gesture of contempt. 'God help us!' he said, then, turning on his heel, he strode back into his flat, closing the door firmly behind him.

By this time Claire had come back on to the landing. She looked from Pippa to the closed door, then back to Pippa, whose face had flushed a dull red at the man's remarks. 'Well, it's a nice flat—

shame about the neighbours!' she said, pulling a face.

'I hope I'm not included in that statement,' said a voice from below, and they looked down to where an auburn-haired girl with a cheerful freckled face was grinning up the stairs at them. 'Hi, there, I'm Sue Robinson. Here, let me give you a hand with this lot.'

Between the three of them they picked up the toys and saucepans, unloaded the rest of Pippa's gear and as quietly as they could carried everything up to her flat. Only when it was all safely installed did they shut the door and relax with a sigh of relief.

When they eventually got round to the long-awaited cup of tea, Sue asked Pippa what ward she was on. 'I've seen you around, but I'm a midwife and obstetrics is a world of its own. I never seem to know exactly where other people work.'

'I'm a third-year student,' explained Pippa. 'I completed my spell on Medical, then a couple of weeks in school; now I'm all set for Casualty.'

'You sound as if you're looking forward to Casualty,' commented Claire.

'I am,' replied Pippa firmly. 'Apparently there isn't a dull moment, or so I've heard.'

'That's true. . .' Sue wrinkled her nose. 'But I can't say I was too keen when I did my stint.'

'Why was that?' Claire looked up with interest.

Sue shrugged. 'I'm not sure really.' She paused reflectively. 'I suppose it had something to do with the fact that you don't have so much individual

patient involvement and you never see the outcome of cases—if you follow my meaning.'

Claire nodded. 'Yes, I do know what you mean,
but from what I've heard Pippa's right when she
says there isn't a dull moment.'

'True,' Sue laughed. 'I can remember when I
was on Casualty I was exhausted at the end of the
day and it cost me a fortune in shoe leather.'

'Why did you choose to go into obstetrics?'
asked Pippa curiously.

'I've always loved babies—I'm part of a very
large family back home in Donegal, there were
always babies around, and somehow it just
seemed the natural thing to do.'

'I wish I could decide what I want.' Claire gave
a sigh and sipped her tea.

'Oh, I'm not going to try and decide until I've
tried everything,' said Pippa.

'I've even wondered recently if nursing really is
for me after all,' said Claire slowly, then, glancing
at the other two girls, she said, 'Do either of you
feel like that?'

Sue shook her head emphatically. 'No, I've
never wanted to do anything else. I always knew
nursing was for me.'

'How about you, Pippa?' asked Claire. 'Are you
another one fulfilling a childhood dream?'

Pippa looked up thoughtfully from the floor,
where she was sitting cross-legged. 'Yes, I suppose
I am, if you put it like that. But when I was very
young I wanted to be a vet. I was always rescuing
animals and birds and bringing them home for
treatment—I drove my mother mad—but I wasn't
sure I'd be able to put animals to sleep, so I

changed my mind to nursing. Now, I couldn't imagine doing anything else. The only aspect that was really getting me down was living in the nurses' home.'

Sue nodded sympathetically. 'Yes, that does get a bit tiresome, I agree, but you'll be all right now you're here. No warden to bother you or check what time you come in.'

Pippa pulled a face. 'No, just an irritable neighbour who doesn't like any form of noise. Who is he, by the way?'

'His name's Richard Lawton.' Sue frowned. 'I think he's a doctor, but, as I said, being in obstetrics I'm not really sure what departments other people work in. Actually he's only here temporarily, according to Tim Barnes who lives in the flat next to me. Tim's a student nurse and a great character,' she added by way of explanation. 'He told me that Richard Lawton is only living here while he's waiting for the builders to finish his new apartment.'

'Well, that's a relief,' said Pippa, climbing to her feet and collecting up the empty mugs. 'He seemed a right stuffed shirt, but I suppose I can put up with him if I know it isn't going to be for too long.'

After the other two girls had gone Pippa set to work and began to sort out her belongings. She worked steadily for three hours, stopping only to grab a sandwich, and by late afternoon she had her flat looking more like home. The bare walls she had covered with posters and prints, their subjects following no specific theme, simply what

had captured her imagination when she had seen
them. The many open shelves she filled with her
collections of books, records, tapes, cuddly animals and pot plants, while on the sofa and chairs
she placed large, brightly coloured squashy cushions. By dusk as the street lights came on in the
avenue below she was almost straight, and as she
lit her two table lamps and pulled the curtains to
shut out the cold December evening she gave a
sigh of satisfaction as she looked round.

She could hardly believe that at last she had a
place of her own. At first it had seemed fun
sharing with the other girls, but as time had passed
she found she had yearned for independence and
freedom from petty restrictions, and when Claire
had told her of the flat that was becoming vacant
at Maple House she had jumped at it. At first she
had been dubious that she would be able to afford
it, but because it was hospital accommodation and
not privately owned and because she was prepared to make any necessary sacrifices she finally
worked out that she would just about be able to
manage.

And later that night when she lay in bed listening to the unfamiliar sounds in her new home she
was certain she had made the right decision. As
far as she could see the only slight aggravation had
come in the shape of her neighbour, Richard
Lawton, but if what Sue had said was right it
didn't even seem as if she would have to put up
with him for long. Her last thought before falling
asleep was that while he remained at Maple House
she wouldn't let his presence bother her, but, at

the same time, she resolved she would do her best to keep out of his way.

The following morning Pippa was awakened by the sound of a water tank filling up. It was still dark, and she lay for a few minutes trying to remember where she was. Then as memory flooded back she leaned over and switched on her table-lamp and peered at the clock beside her bed. With a start she sat up and, picking up the clock, stared at it in disbelief, then shook it. For some reason the alarm hadn't gone off, and she was certain she had set it the night before. She was now at least half an hour late, and with a groan she jumped out of bed and, grabbing a towel, headed for the shower.

Somehow, by eating a slice of toast and drinking a cup of coffee while she dressed, she managed to make up some lost time. A glance out of the window had revealed ice patterns on the outside of the pane, although, inside, the flat mercifully was deliciously warm, heated by several radiators.

At last she was ready, and, pulling on her coat and scarf, she let herself out of the flat. The rest of the house was silent, and as she hurried downstairs she found herself wondering about the other occupants and what time they started work. She stepped out of the front door and was struck by the biting cold. Turning up her collar, she hurried across the forecourt to her car.

It still wasn't quite light, and as she tried to get her key in the lock she prayed that the lock wasn't frozen. The key, however, turned, and she opened the door, then paused to bid the milkman a good morning as he came up the drive. Her breath hung in the frosty morning air and with a little shiver she slipped into the front seat and fastened her seatbelt.

The car started at the third attempt, and with a sigh of relief and a quick glance at her watch, which was just visible in the light from the dashboard, Pippa saw that she just had time to get to the hospital before her shift began. Switching on the headlights, she pulled out of the forecourt and on to the main road.

Whitford General Hospital was on the far side of the town, and as Pippa joined the other early-morning motorists she felt her apprehension growing. She had already been warned that work in Casualty would be very different from what she had come to expect on the wards, and she found herself hoping she would be able to stand the pace and that she wouldn't be squeamish at what she might see.

She drew up at a set of traffic-lights and in the glow from her dipped headlights she caught sight of a small bundle on the pavement against the wall. As the lights changed and she pulled away she noticed that the bundle was moving. With an anxious glance in her mirror to check that there was nothing behind her, she drew forward so that she was well clear of the lights, then pulled over. Setting her hazard indicators, she scrambled out of the car and hurried back to the small dark shape.

As she approached she heard a whining sound, and with an exclamation she bent down and saw that the bundle was in fact a very young black Labrador puppy. It was shaking with cold and fright, and when Pippa picked it up it snuggled into the warm wool of her coat.

'Oh, you poor little thing!' she whispered as it nuzzled its wet nose into the palm of her hand. 'But wherever have you come from?' She glanced round, but there were no residential buildings nearby, only shops and offices still in darkness waiting for their staff to arrive. She hesitated, wondering if the dog had been abandoned or whether it had escaped. Then she remembered that the police station was only a few streets away, and after an anxious glance at her watch she walked back to her car with the puppy still cuddled in her arms.

She settled the dog on a rug on the back seat, then climbed into the car, started the engine and pulled out into the traffic again. She quickly found she had underestimated the distance to the police station, just as she had forgotten the complicated system of one-way streets that she needed to negotiate to get there.

By the time she arrived, had found somewhere to park and carried the puppy into Reception, she was running hopelessly late.

The sergeant on duty was very kind, but he insisted she stayed and filled in a form.

'Can I phone later and see if he's been claimed?' asked Pippa anxiously as the sergeant picked up the puppy.

'Of course you can. He's a grand little chap, isn't he?' The policeman smiled, and Pippa felt a little pang as the puppy rested its nose on its oversized paws and gazed dolefully at her.

Then as she caught sight of the clock above the

desk she gave a start and rushed from the building, knowing there was now no way she could hope to get to work on time.

When she reached the hospital she had to drive round the staff car park beside the casualty unit twice before she found a parking-space. Then at last when she finally presented herself at the sister's office she was a good fifteen minutes late.

Mercifully there was no sign of Sister, and she was met by a staff nurse, who greeted her with raised eyebrows.

'Nurse Ward?' she asked, and when Pippa nodded she went on, 'We'd almost given you up, you know.'

'I'm very sorry.' Pippa was quite breathless with hurrying. 'But I found a dog in the road and I had to take it to the police station.'

The staff nurse sighed. 'Well, never mind, you're here now. I'm Karen Taylor. Sister is over the other side at the moment in Accident and Emergency; they've had an RTA in—Road Traffic Accident,' she explained when she saw Pippa's blank look. 'The changing-room's through there; get yourself sorted out and report back here to me when you're ready. Oh, and it's Philippa, isn't it?'

'Yes, but I like to be called Pippa.'

Karen Taylor smiled. 'Very well, Pippa it is, among ourselves, but Nurse Ward in front of the patients. You'll find it's pretty strict around here. I warn you, the CO is an absolute stickler for protocol and efficiency. Now hurry along and get changed.'

Pippa nodded and, turning sharply, almost collided with someone coming into the office.

'Oh, I'm sorry. . .' she said, then she stopped and stared up in dismay at the tall dark-haired man before her.

'Oh, Pippa,' said Staff Nurse Taylor, 'this is Dr Lawton, our casualty officer.'

CHAPTER TWO

HE FROWNED, and Pippa gaped at him, hardly
able to believe her eyes. Staff Nurse had said he
was the CO, but surely fate couldn't be that cruel.
She tried to speak, but found that her mouth had
gone dry, then she realised that he too didn't seem
too happy to find her in his unit.

Raising his eyebrows, he looked enquiringly at
Karen Taylor, ignoring Pippa, who noticed irrele-
vantly that today he wasn't wearing his glasses.
His grey eyes, however, were like flint, and she
swallowed as she waited in silence.

'Nurse Ward is our new student,' said Karen by
way of explanation.

'Well, she'll have to keep better time than this if
she wants to be part of my team.' His tone was
clipped and as bleak as the expression in his eyes.

'I'm sure she won't be late again,' said Karen,
then, turning to Pippa, she added, 'Hurry up now
and get yourself ready. It'll be really busy soon
and we need every pair of hands we can get.'

Pippa hurried from the office, her head down as
she passed Dr Lawton so that she couldn't see his
face, but she was only too aware of his disapprov-
ing expression. Then she heard Karen say,
'They're ready for you now, Dr Lawton. It's a
particularly nasty RTA. A middle-aged man with a
crushed thorax—impact from the steering-wheel.'

Pippa closed the door of the changing-room

behind her and couldn't hear any more. Briefly she leaned against the door and closed her eyes. Why, oh, why, of all the doctors in Whitford General, did Dr Richard Lawton have to be the CO? She had taken an instant dislike to him the previous day at Maple House, thinking him rude and arrogant, and now, today, somehow she had managed to get off on the wrong foot from the very first moment by being late.

With a sigh she opened her eyes and looked round the changing-room with its rows of lockers and coat pegs, then, taking a deep breath, she took off her coat and began to change into the crisp blue and white uniform she had brought with her. Her long hair she had already plaited into the neat mane-like style she wore for work, and when she was ready she secured her white cap with a couple of hair-grips. Then, straightening her shoulders, she smoothed down her uniform, opened the door and stepped out into the corridor.

There was no sign of the staff nurse, and suddenly Pippa felt very apprehensive. What would be expected of her on Casualty? Already she had heard the words 'efficiency' and 'working as part of a team', and she knew a moment's panic as she wondered whether she would cope with the unknown. She had enjoyed her previous work on the wards, but she knew this was going to be very different.

She made her way back to Sister's office, but found it empty, then as she stood wondering what she should do next she heard someone call her name. She looked up sharply and saw Karen

Taylor beckoning to her from a cubicle farther down the corridor.

'Come here, Nurse Ward,' she said. 'I want you to put clean draw-sheets and a blanket on each of the couches in these cubicles. Get your supplies from the linen cupboard, and by the time you've finished I should be back, then I'll show you round.'

'Are you going somewhere?' Pippa looked bewildered.

'Only to the other side of the unit. I'm needed over there in Accident and Emergency with this RTA.'

'So what are these cubicles for?' Pippa indicated the row of cubicles behind her.

'These are dressing cubicles for Category Three and Four patients, in other words the not so seriously injured, or the walking wounded, as we call them. Don't worry,' Karen added kindly, 'I know it's all a bit confusing, but I'll explain everything later.' With that she was gone, leaving Pippa to collect her sheets and blankets and prepare the cubicles for the morning's patients.

She worked steadily until she had prepared all the couches and stowed the dirty linen away into green plastic bags ready to be picked up by the laundry van. Then, feeling quite satisfied with herself, she stepped out into the corridor, and because there was no sign of any other member of staff she made her way to the reception area.

In spite of the early hour there were already several patients waiting in the rows of chairs that faced the large main reception desk. The receptionist, a blonde-haired girl with a bright smile, looked up at Pippa as she approached the desk.

'Hello, there,' she said. 'I'm Gina—you're new, aren't you?'

Pippa nodded. 'Yes, it's my first day, I'm Pippa Ward.'

Gina smiled. 'What a super name for a nurse—I knew a Dr Stitch once.'

Pippa laughed, liking Gina immediately, then, leaning forward so that the patients couldn't hear, she said, 'Are there always patients in here?'

Gina nodded. 'Yes—at all times, day and night. I don't think there's ever a time when Cas isn't busy.' Then, looking with interest at Pippa, she said, 'Have you met the rest of the team yet?'

'Not really.' Pippa shook her head. 'I'm waiting for Staff Nurse Taylor, she's going to show me round. Oh, and I've met Dr Lawton.'

'And what did you think of him?' Gina looked up at her from under her lashes.

'Well. . .' Pippa hesitated.

'Not too impressed, eh? He can be a bit forbidding, but he's a terrific doctor.'

'Let's just say we got off to a bad start,' Pippa replied, then jumped as the double doors were suddenly flung open and a young man appeared. His appearance was scruffy and dishevelled, and in his arms he carried a young child. Wildly he glanced around, then as his gaze fell on Pippa she saw relief in his eyes and to her dismay he began to hurry across the floor towards her.

'She's having an attack,' he said abruptly, thrusting the child towards her. 'It's worse than usual and I don't know what to do.'

Pippa automatically held out her arms, then staggered at the unexpected weight of the child.

The little girl's breathing was noisy and laboured.
Her eyes were closed and her fair hair was damp
and sticking to her face, which appeared almost
transparent, the blue veins clearly visible beneath
the pale skin.

Pippa felt a moment's panic and glanced wildly
round Reception, but there was no sign of any
other staff except Gina. As her eyes met Gina's,
the receptionist stood up and hurried round to the
front of the desk.

'They're all in Accident and Emergency,' she
muttered. 'I'll get someone; you take the child into
one of the examination-rooms.' She pointed
behind Pippa, then she was gone, leaving her with
the frantic young man and the child.

'You'll have to do something. . .' said the man,
and the sound of his voice seemed to galvanise
Pippa into action. She turned, and, crossing
Reception, was vaguely aware that one of the
waiting patients called after her, saying it was his
turn and asking how much longer did they expect
him to wait.

She ignored him, hoping Gina would sort him
out on her return, and, pushing open the swing
doors of the large examination-room with her hip,
she carried the child into the room. A quick glance
revealed two examination couches and a room
packed with equipment.

She headed for one of the couches and as gently
as she could placed the child on to her side.

'It's her asthma—she's always getting attacks,
but this one was worse than usual.' The man had
followed her and was standing directly behind
her, trying to look over her shoulder at the child,

who by this time was wheezing badly. 'I didn't know what to do. . .her mother wasn't home from work. . .'

'Are you her father?' asked Pippa quickly as instinctively she leaned the little girl forward and began rubbing her back.

'No. . .her mum's me girlfriend. . .she works nights in an old people's home. I look after the kids. . .'

'There are more than one?'

'Yes, there's Ben, he was still asleep. He'll be all right till I get back.'

Pippa swallowed, uncertain what to do. Instinct told her to tell this man to get back to the other child as quickly as he could before any harm befell him, but she also knew that the staff would need to question him about the little girl. She looked at the child. 'What's her name?' she asked.

'Carly.'

'And what does Carly use for her asthma?'

'Becotide Rotacaps, the one hundreds.' He said it with enough certainty to convince Pippa, then added, 'She's had a go with them this morning, but they didn't seem to work.'

Suddenly the little girl began coughing and opened her eyes. Turning her head, she stared up at Pippa in bewilderment and distress.

Pippa came to a decision. 'Right, Mr. . . Mr. . .'

'Peters,' he told her.

'Mr Peters. . . I want you to go back into Reception, phone Carly's mother at work, explain what's happened. Tell her to make arrangements for Ben, then to come here as soon as she can.'

He nodded and disappeared through the double

doors without argument, leaving Pippa to soothe and calm the frightened little girl as best she could.

She didn't have long to wait; only minutes later the doors opened again and a middle-aged woman in a sister's uniform appeared. She was closely followed by Karen Taylor.

'What's going on, Nurse?' asked Sister after a keen look at Carly, who by this time had got over her coughing spasm and was lying quietly on her side clutching Pippa's hand.

'This is Carly,' said Pippa, and went on to explain what had happened.

'And where's Mr Peters?' asked Karen as Sister began setting up a nebuliser.

'He's in Reception phoning her mother,' replied Pippa.

'I don't suppose we know her medication,' said a voice from the doorway, and Pippa stiffened as without turning she recognised Dr Lawton's voice.

'Yes,' she said quietly, still without turning. 'It's Becotide Rotacaps, one hundred micrograms.'

She was briefly aware of the look that passed between Karen and the sister, then they all seemed to swing into action and Pippa somehow got pushed to the back of the room.

A little while later Mr Peters returned and was reassured by Dr Lawton that Carly's asthma attack was well under control. When Carly's mother arrived Karen Taylor had just told Pippa to go to Sister's office, but as she left the examination-room Mr Peters suddenly called after her.

'Oh, Nurse, thanks for what you did,' he said.

Pippa flushed as she felt Dr Lawton's cool gaze upon her.

'I didn't do anything really,' she said, embarrassed that everyone was suddenly looking at her.

'Well, you were very good,' said Mr Peters, and turned to Carly's mother, obviously to explain Pippa's part in the drama. Pippa not waiting to hear more, fled to Sister's office.

She didn't have long to wait, as Sister joined her almost immediately. She was small and wiry with a ruddy complexion, crisp dark hair and a no-nonsense approach. She came straight to the point.

'Philippa Ward, isn't it? I'm Sister Rose Gould. We're pleased to have you on Casualty. As I'm sure you've already found out, the work here is very different from anything you've done before.' She stared keenly at Pippa, seeming to take in every detail of her appearance but not giving her a chance to speak. 'I'm afraid you were rather flung in at the deep end back there. I can assure you that doesn't usually happen on a student's first few moments in Casualty. On the other hand, every moment you're here you have to be prepared for any eventuality.' She glanced sharply at Pippa and something in her gaze warned Pippa what was to follow. 'Normally on your arrival you'd be shown around, then given some sort of routine job to acclimatise you, but you didn't seem to be around when the shift started this morning.'

Pippa shifted uncomfortably, expecting a reprimand. She opened her mouth in an attempt to explain what had happened, then realised that Sister's eyes were twinkling. 'It's all right, Nurse Ward, Staff told me what happened. A dog, wasn't it?'

Pippa nodded. 'Yes, a Labrador pup. I think it had been abandoned, and I took it to the police station. Of course, that made me horribly late. I'm very sorry, Sister,' she added.

'We'll overlook it this time, although I'm afraid Dr Lawton wasn't too impressed. You mustn't let it happen again; he's a stickler for punctuality.'

Pippa nodded. There it was again, another reference to the high standards Richard Lawton expected from his team. Sister Gould went on to question Pippa about her personal details and her accommodation, then she picked up some folders from her desk. 'Now, let's see if we can get you properly organised. Staff Nurse Taylor is going to show you round and explain how we function, so we'll go and see if we can find her.' She crossed the room, opened the door, then stood back for Pippa to precede her and almost as an afterthought she said, 'Oh, and by the way, Nurse, well done over the way you handled the asthma case. You did very well under the circumstances.' She smiled, and Pippa suddenly felt ridiculously pleased.

'Oh, thank you, Sister! I imagined I'd done everything wrong.'

'You didn't quite get it all right,' she replied crisply. 'You shouldn't have let Mr Peters go off to the phone on his own. He might have disappeared before we'd had a chance to get Carly's details.'

Pippa wanted to ask her what she should have done, but by that time they were back in the reception area and Sister Gould was immediately in demand.

Karen Taylor was checking some registration

details with Gina and another student, but when she caught sight of Pippa she smiled, and, glancing at the fob watch on the front of her uniform, said, 'Right, Nurse Ward, time for your official introduction to Casualty.' She looked round. 'Seeing that we're in Reception I should think it could be a good place to start.'

Pippa listened intently as Karen went on to explain that the two sections of Casualty, the dressing cubicles or the side for the less seriously injured patients, and the Accident and Emergency side, or A and E as it was referred to by the staff, were separated by Reception, the large waiting area, the stores and the nurses' station.

'Everyone who comes into Casualty under his own steam has to report to Reception and fill in a registration form, or, if their injuries render them incapable of doing that, we ask a relative to do it for them,' said Karen. 'They're then asked to wait and cases are dealt with in rotation.'

'Supposing a case is very urgent?' asked Pippa, looking round at the waiting area, which was already filling up with what appeared to be a wide cross-section of the general public.

'The very urgent cases usually come by ambulance to the other side—A and E. But there are, of course, occasions when someone is brought in by car or even on foot who requires immediate attention. These are very often cardiac cases, and obviously they're dealt with straight away either in the resuscitation-room, or if that's full, in one of the treatment-rooms. As I explained to you earlier, the cubicles you helped to prepare are used for minor dressings.' By this time they had left Reception and were approaching the row of cubicles. Pippa could see that several of them were occupied, and, as they approached, a doctor emerged from one of them. She was writing something on a drug sheet attached to a clipboard. She looked up and nodded vaguely in their direction.

'That's Dr Hannah Scott. I'll introduce you properly later,' said Karen. 'She looks a bit harassed at the moment.' As she spoke they heard the sound of loud voices coming from behind the curtains of one of the cubicles. Karen pulled a face. 'Another domestic dispute, by the sounds of it. You'll have to get used to those, they happen all the time. It's surprising how people think Casualty's a good place to sort out their differences.'

They walked away from the cubicles, then paused in what appeared to be an administration area. Two nurses were sorting notes and one was writing a name on to a large blackboard.

'Every patient is listed on the blackboard together with the nature of their complaint and the number of the cubicle we put them in,' said Karen, then added, 'This is most important and is constantly being updated as patients are discharged and new ones arrive.'

'Isn't it written in a book as well?' asked Pippa, who was thinking that details could so easily be lost from a blackboard.

Karen shook her head. 'No, not in a book, but on the registration card which the patient has filled in at Reception and which they bring with them when they're called. The cards are later filed away with all the information on that patient.'

Pippa nodded, then asked, 'Does every patient see a doctor?'

'Yes, once they've been allocated to a cubicle the nursing staff prepare the patient as much as possible by cleaning up any mess, removing clothing from around wounds—that sort of thing—then the patient waits for the doctor. Sometimes it can be a long wait, depending on what else is happening at the time. Accident and Emergency always takes precedence, and sometimes all the doctors are over there for hours on end, especially if we have a particularly bad traffic accident from the motorway.'

'What do the nurses do while the patients are waiting to see the doctor?' Suddenly Pippa was very interested and wanted to find out as much as she could about this branch of nursing that looked as if it was going to be very different from what she had become used to on the wards.

Karen gave a short laugh. 'It sounds as if there's a lot of waiting around, doesn't it? But in reality it isn't a bit like that. In fact there usually isn't a moment to breathe. When you aren't actually attending to patients there are always relatives to contend with—and, believe me, Pippa, a good deal of your time will be spent with relatives, either taking details from them, reassuring them or consoling them.'

'Consoling them?' Pippa looked anxious.

'Yes, very often on A and E we have a patient who's dead on arrival or who dies in the treatment or resuscitation-room. Usually the relatives have been informed by the police that there's been an accident and arrive at Casualty hoping to see the patient sitting up in bed with not too much wrong with them. Instead they find themselves being asked to identify a body. The shock is tremendous, and it's down to us to lessen the trauma of it as much as we can.' Karen threw Pippa a glance as she spoke. 'Are you beginning to understand the importance of the role you'll be playing while you're with our team?'

'Yes, I think so,' Pippa nodded slowly. 'I had no idea so much was involved.'

'I think it takes a special kind of person to do casualty work,' Karen went on. 'Now where did we get to? Oh, yes, patients waiting in cubicles for a doctor. . .well, first the doctor examines them to assess the degree of injury, then he or she decides what procedures are to be carried out—maybe it will be X-rays, blood tests, or perhaps only a simple dressing is required. If that's the case the doctor will do any stitching and usually the dressings will be done by us nurses. If X-rays are required we'll escort the patient to the X-ray department. Sometimes, usually on the A and E side, the doctor may call for a consultant to see a patient, then, more often than not, the patient will be admitted to a ward. There are several procedures that are then carried out, but we won't go into those today. I think I've probably told you enough for you to be going on with.'

Pippa nodded thankfully. Her head was reeling from all that Karen had told her, and she was convinced she would never remember any of it.

'Now, I think it's time for your coffee break,' said Karen. 'After that we'll go over and see Dr

Lawton on A and E and you can see what goes on over there.'

At the mention of his name Pippa felt her heart sink, and while she drank her coffee she found herself dreading her visit to his efficient, highly organised domain.

CHAPTER THREE

IT WAS every bit as bad as Pippa had imagined: a
sterile, highly powered unit which appeared to be
run on dictatorial lines. When Pippa arrived with
Karen they found Dr Lawton in the large treatment-room. Together with a staff nurse and an
enrolled nurse he was bending over a patient. It
looked to Pippa as if he was removing pieces of
glass from the young man's legs. This assumption
proved correct, for as the staff nurse came to collect
fresh dressings from a cupboard near to where
they were standing she whispered that the patient
had fallen through a plate-glass window.

Momentarily Pippa felt her head swim, then she
gritted her teeth and forced herself to look at his
injuries. It would never do for her to pass out on
her first visit to A and E. She shuddered as she
briefly allowed herself to imagine the look of
contempt that would surely appear on Dr
Lawton's face if she were to do so. Then she willed
herself to concentrate.

The patient, barely out of his teens, lay white-
faced and obviously very much in a state of shock
as the three members of staff worked on him. His
trousers and shirt had been cut away, to reveal
appalling flesh wounds to his legs and upper
torso. Blood-soaked swabs surrounded him, while
Dr Lawton bent across him, probing in a gaping
thigh wound with a pair of forceps.

He glanced in their direction only once, and when Karen asked if they might watch he nodded abruptly and without speaking carried on with his work.

Pippa watched intently as he removed one sliver of glass after another, then quite against her will she found herself studying him instead of what he was doing. As if mesmerised she watched his strong hands encased in thin latex gloves, the long fingers as they gripped the forceps and gently but firmly extracted the lethal shards of glass. Then her gaze flickered to the lean contours of his face, for the first time taking note of the straight nose and slightly flaring nostrils above a well-defined mouth and firm square jaw. He was wearing his glasses again for the intricate job he was doing, and the edge of the heavy rims hid the expression in those cool grey eyes. His white coat was open, revealing an immaculate striped shirt and pressed trousers, while a stethoscope protruded from one pocket. Almost as if he sensed Pippa's scrutiny he suddenly looked up, and his eyes met hers.

'It's no good standing over there, Nurse,' he said. 'You'll never see anything. Come over here and watch what I'm doing.'

Pippa felt the colour stain her cheeks. It was almost as if he had known she had been looking at him and not the patient, then she felt Karen give her a little push and she crossed to the couch.

For the next ten minutes or so she watched intently while Dr Lawton removed the final few pieces of glass, then with the assistance of one of the nurses prepared to stitch the wound. Once, Pippa looked over her shoulder and saw that

Karen had disappeared, and she had the peculiar feeling of having been abandoned, then, as she was silently telling herself not to be so stupid, she felt someone touch her hand. She jumped, and, looking down, found the patient was trying to attract her attention. He had been sedated, his mouth was obviously very dry and he was having difficulty speaking. She bent her head towards him away from Dr Lawton and what he was doing.

'What is it?' she asked as she looked down into a pair of frightened blue eyes.

'How. . .how much longer?' he whispered.

'Not long now,' she replied, taking his hand and gripping it tightly. She didn't really have a clue how much longer Dr Lawton would take, but she felt she had to try and reassure the boy, who wasn't much younger than herself. 'Have you got anyone with you?' she asked a moment later as he winced with sudden pain and gripped her hand more tightly.

He shook his head. 'My boss was here. . . I did it at work. . .he's gone now, but they've phoned my mum.'

'I expect she'll be here soon,' said Pippa comfortingly.

'Is it too bad, Nurse?' he asked, trying to lift his head to see what Dr Lawton was doing.

'No, you'll be as right as rain when the doctor's finished with you.' She tried to sound positive, but she felt a pang as she saw a tear slide down his cheek.

'If you've finished, Nurse, perhaps you'd like to watch this suturing.' Richard Lawton had straightened up and was peering at her over his glasses.

She started guiltily and, extricating her hand from the patient's, moved down the couch so that she could watch the suturing.

As she followed the neat deft movements of Dr Lawton's hands she wondered why it was that everything that this man said set her on edge, and came to the conclusion that her first impression of him had been correct. She now realised, however, that her earlier plan to keep well out of his way just wasn't going to be feasible, for it seemed that for the next ten weeks she was going to be seeing quite a bit of him.

Even before he had finished, other emergencies arrived at the unit; a woman with a suspected perforated appendix and an elderly man with an eye injury.

Pippa watched, fascinated, as the team went into a well-rehearsed routine and coped with each incident, then, before she knew it, Karen had returned and taken her back to Reception.

She spent the rest of the morning until lunch-time allocating patients to cubicles after they had given their details to Gina.

In the staff canteen, Claire, and Mandy, another of her student friends, were having their lunch, so Pippa bought herself some hot soup and a couple of bread rolls and joined them.

They had all started on new wards that morning and were eager to share their experiences. Claire was on a surgical ward and had apparently already fallen foul of the sister, and Mandy had started on Gynae.

'How about you, Pippa, how do you like

Casualty?' asked Claire as she toyed with her salad.

'I think I'm going to like the work—it's so different and varied—and it seems as if there's never a dull moment, as I thought. But you'll never guess who the registrar is.'

Claire frowned and shook her head.

'Only my charming neighbour—the one who complained about the noise yesterday.'

'Oh, him, the one with charisma,' said Claire sarcastically, while Mandy looked up with sudden interest.

'Yes, him. I nearly died when I saw him this morning, and, to make matters worse, I was late. It seems that's unforgivable in Casualty. Honestly, it sounds to me as if the place is run like Alcatraz!'

'You mean the sister's a tyrant?' asked Mandy.

'She can't be any worse than mine,' Claire sniffed.

Pippa shook her head. 'No, it isn't Sister; in fact she's rather nice. It's him—the CO, or registrar, or whatever he calls himself—he seems to be in charge, and when he barks everyone jumps.'

'You'll just have to try and keep out of his way, Pippa,' said Mandy with a grin.

'Well, that was what I thought when I first met him at Maple House.' Pippa pulled a face. 'But then I hadn't bargained for having to work with him as well. The trouble is, he's one of those people who unnerve me, and I know I'll do everything wrong when he's around.' She set her spoon down and looked up, then paused. 'Oh, dear, talk of the devil—don't look now, but he's just come in.'

Surreptitiously the three girls watched as Dr Lawton collected his lunch from the self-service bar and looked round for a table. But instead of joining a group of his colleagues who were sitting in the coveted window-seats he carried his tray to an empty table some distance from the three girls and sat alone.

'He doesn't look too bad,' said Claire.

'You can't go by looks,' declared Pippa firmly, and picked up her spoon again.

'When do we get to see this new bedsit?' asked Mandy, changing the subject.

'When you like,' replied Pippa. 'How about coming over tonight? We could get a pizza takeaway.'

'OK, I'll bring some plonk and we'll christen the flat,' said Mandy. 'How about you, Claire?'

'Hmm?' Claire didn't appear to have heard them.

'Claire! What are you staring at?' asked Pippa.

'Your registrar. . .you know, he's really quite dishy. . .if he were to take his glasses off and have his hair cut in a modern style. . .'

'Well, I don't think so,' said Pippa. 'He certainly isn't my type. Do you know, I haven't even seen him smile?'

'I quite like the mean and moody type.' Mandy pursed her lips into a reflective pout.

'Huh!' Pippa stood up. 'Mean being the operative word, and it's what he'll be if I'm late back from lunch. See you girls later. . . OK?'

Pippa spent the remainder of her shift assisting Karen and the other nurse, Julie Acland, with dressings in Casualty. These were varied, ranging from minor cuts, burns and scalds to another asthma case, a baby with a severe chest infection who was later admitted to the children's ward and a woman with pelvic pain who had to be referred to a gynaecologist. Pippa relaxed and became deeply involved after hearing that Dr Lawton was working in A and E and Dr Scott was dealing with the walking wounded.

'You've done well, for your first day,' said Karen as they prepared to go off duty.

'I feel rather confused,' replied Pippa. 'There's so much to remember.'

'Don't worry, you'll soon get the hang of it. You certainly seem to have a feel for it—Casualty isn't everyone's cup of tea. But don't forget, Pippa, if you have any worries, either at work or of a personal nature, please come and talk things over with me.'

'Thanks, Karen.' Pippa was grateful she had a sympathetic staff nurse in charge of her—it made all the difference, as she knew only too well from her experience on the other wards. As she turned to leave the office to change into her outdoor clothes she paused as Karen suddenly called her back.

'Oh, by the way, Pippa, on Casualty we usually work one week on the dressing side and the next on A and E. But to start with we want to get you familiar with both sections, so tomorrow you'll be over on A and E.'

Pippa's dismay must have shown on her face, for Karen looked keenly at her. 'Is anything wrong?' she asked.

'Not really. . .'

'You're not worrying about working for Dr Lawton, are you?'

'Well——' Pippa hesitated, uncertain how to put into words that she felt intimidated by the registrar.

But before she had a chance to say any more Karen intervened. 'You mustn't mind him, he's a workaholic, very ambitious, and he thinks everyone else in his team should feel exactly the same way about their work as he does. Just do your best—and, Pippa. . .whatever you do don't be late again tomorrow.'

'Don't worry,' Pippa pulled a face, 'there's no fear of that!'

When she left the hospital it was still bitingly cold, and she thought to herself that there would probably be another frost that evening. It seemed unusual for it to be so cold so early in the winter, and just for a moment she found herself wondering if there could possibly be a white Christmas. She had spent much of her childhood growing up in Australia and had consequently never seen snow at Christmas, although it had long been her wish to do so.

She wasn't particularly looking forward to Christmas that year as both her parents were on a visit to their friends in Perth and wouldn't be back until early in the New Year. Pippa had volunteered to work as she knew most of the other students were desperate to go home, and from her previous experience of her first Christmas at Whitford it was fun on the wards over the festive season. That, however, had been before she'd known she would be on Casualty. She wondered now if she had

been too hasty in her offer; the thought of
Christmas in Accident and Emergency with Dr
Richard Lawton held about as much appeal as a
wet Bank Holiday under canvas.

On her way home she stopped at the supermarket and stocked up with food and other supplies,
and on a sudden impulse bought a large bottle of
Lambrusco as she remembered that Claire and
some of the others would be coming to see her
bedsit later that evening.

She parked her car on the forecourt of Maple
House and fleetingly wondered if Richard Lawton
was home, then decided that he probably worked
double shifts in his beloved unit.

The first person she saw as she stepped into the
hall was Sue Robinson, who was coming from the
large communal kitchen which they were all at
liberty to use if they wished. In her arms she
carried a large bundle of clean laundry. Behind her
was a tall thin young man with tight curly hair and
a worried expression.

'Hi, Pippa, how did your day go?' asked Sue
brightly, then, not waiting for an answer, she said,
'Oh, this is Tim—Tim Barnes. He's in Flat One.'

'Hello, Tim,' Pippa smiled a greeting, wondering briefly why he looked so fed up. Then, turning
to Sue, she said, 'It wasn't too bad, I suppose, but
I'm glad to finish—my head is reeling!'

'You need to unwind,' said Sue firmly.

'I agree.' Then, as a thought struck her, Pippa
added, 'I've some people coming over later for a
drink; why don't you join us? Both of you, of
course,' she added, looking past Sue to Tim, who
continued to look gloomy.

'Thank you, we'd love to come,' said Sue, answering for them both, then, as Tim shook his head and began to protest, she said, 'Don't be silly, Tim, of course you're coming. There's no way you're sitting in that flat on your own tonight.'

Pippa looked enquiringly from one to the other, but Tim merely lowered his head and began kicking the edge of the stair with a scuffed trainer, and it was left to Sue to explain.

'Tim heard today that he's failed his finals,' she said.

'Oh, how awful!' exclaimed Pippa, aghast. She really couldn't think of anything worse, and it reminded her of the fact that her own finals were now less than a year away. For a moment she couldn't think of anything to say, then haltingly she said, 'Well, never mind, I'm sure you'll pass second time round.'

An awkward silence followed, then Tim said quietly, 'That was second time. . .one more shot, and if I mess it up that time, that's me out.' With an attempt at a nonchalant shrug that didn't fool either girl he turned and walked away.

Sue watched him go, then turned back to Pippa. 'Poor old Tim, he's taken it really hard this time. He's the last one of his group to qualify.'

'I can't think of anything worse,' said Pippa. 'Do you think he'll make it next time?'

Sue shrugged. 'Who knows? From what I've heard he's a good nurse, but he goes to pieces over exams. Maybe it'll be that he's one of those who have to accept that nursing isn't for him— like your friend Claire was saying yesterday.'

As Pippa climbed slowly up to her flat she found herself wondering about Claire. It had come as something as a shock to hear her friend voice her doubts about nursing, because Pippa had never doubted her own vocation and had never heard Claire do so before. She let herself into her flat and with a sigh of relief dumped her shopping and flopped down on to the sofa, kicking off her shoes and wriggling her toes in unrestrained bliss.

Pippa and Claire had started their training together; two very raw recruits meeting for the first time on the steps of the nurses' home, only to find they had not only been allocated rooms on the same floor but that the rooms were adjoining. A strong friendship had grown between the two girls, each helping the other with the nightmares of homesickness, first experiences on the wards, studying, and the dreaded end-of-term exams and assessments.

There had of course been the lighter side, and they had lived their student days to the full with parties, discos and outings. They had also had their share of relationships, with medical students, housemen and ambulance drivers, but neither had become seriously involved. Pippa had made up her mind that she wouldn't allow any relationship to become serious, at least until she had finished her training, and she knew that Claire had felt the same way. Now, however, she found herself wondering if Claire's comments about nursing had been anything to do with a certain paramedic whom she had been seeing rather a lot.

As she showered and changed and prepared the flat for her friends' arrival, dimming the lights and putting out a selection of peanuts and crisps, Pippa decided she would tackle Claire on the subject just as soon as she had the opportunity. The thought of Claire giving up on the training and leaving Whitford General was almost more than she could bear.

It seemed the word had spread about Pippa's new home, and by seven o'clock there were no fewer than eight crammed into her bedsit. Claire and Mandy were despatched to the nearest take-away, returning with thick wedges of pizza with delicious toppings. Others had brought wine which Pippa poured into a variety of glasses and mugs, and someone produced a tape of the Pet Shop Boys.

As Pippa inserted the tape into her cassette player an image of Richard Lawton's moody features flitted across her mind and her finger hovered over the volume control button. For a moment she was tempted to turn it up full. She hesitated and glanced round the crowded room. The sofa was packed, some sat on the floor on her cushions and a girl perched on the table. Two others had just arrived, and it looked as if the entire occupants of Maple House had turned out to christen her flat. But there was one resident missing, and it was the absence of that one that decided her to keep the volume down.

Sue had dragged Tim Barnes along, poured him a mugful of Lambrusco, and he was sitting in a corner quietly drowning his sorrows. Claire had her paramedic, Tony, with her and was sitting on the floor at his feet, her head resting against his legs as he lounged in a corner of the sofa.

Suddenly Pippa felt very happy—she loved impromptu parties, and now, being in her own flat surrounded by her friends and new neighbours, she felt as if she was walking on air.

Then somehow—she wasn't sure how it happened—but someone changed the tape, the volume was increased and the sounds of Madonna filled the air.

'What's up, Pippa?' It was Claire at her elbow, and she turned sharply, almost spilling her drink.

'What do you mean?' she asked.

'You look worried, and there's no need—it's a smashing party.'

'I was just thinking about Dr Lawton.'

'Oh, him. . .what are you worrying about him for?'

'Well, the music is a bit loud.' She looked across the room to the cassette player on the top of the bookcase, hopelessly out of her reach now beyond a sea of bodies.

Claire shrugged. 'Perhaps you ought to go and invite him in—then he couldn't say anything, could he?'

'Oh, Claire, I couldn't! He's my boss, and he certainly wouldn't mix with the likes of us students.'

'Well, he'll just have to put up with it, then, won't he?' Claire turned away as Tony leaned forward to whisper something to her, and Pippa knew she'd lost her friend's attention.

Uneasily she bit her lip, then, trying to put the thought of her boss right out of her mind, and thinking hopefully that there was always the possibility that he might be out, she took another sip of her wine, then turned her head as Tracey, another of her student friends, called her name.

'What's this I hear about you being late on your first morning on Cas?' she asked, and one or two others turned to hear Pippa's reply.

Ruefully she nodded. 'Yes, I'm afraid it's true.' As she spoke she suddenly remembered the Labrador pup and that she had told the police sergeant she would phone and see if he had been claimed.

She looked round for somewhere to put her mug but couldn't find a spare corner anywhere, so, still clutching it, she slipped out of the flat, closing the door behind her. It was cold on the landing after the heat in the flat and there was still that faint elusive scent of honeysuckle. It was not, however, very much quieter, and with a nervous glance at the closed door of Richard Lawton's flat Pippa hurried downstairs to the pay-phone which she had earlier noticed on the wall in the passage to the kitchen.

The passage was only dimly lit, and, setting down her mug on a small console table beneath the phone, she fumbled through the directory, screwing up her eyes as she tried to find the number of the local police station.

The sergeant she had spoken to in the morning wasn't on duty and the one who answered didn't sound as helpful, but eventually he went off to see what he could find out.

Pippa leaned against the wall, suddenly feeling very tired as the events of the last two days caught up with her. With one hand she released the band that secured her hair and shaking her head she allowed her hair to tumble over her shoulders, then as she heard the sergeant's voice again she tightened her grip on the receiver.

Anxiously she listened, then a smile crossed her features as the sergeant, who seemed less surly now, told her that the puppy had been claimed by a small boy and his mother during the morning. Apparently he had chewed his way out of his pen and slipped out of the house unnoticed, but was none the worse for his adventure.

'Oh, I'm so pleased he was all right, even if he did cause me a lot of trouble,' she laughed.

'Trouble, miss? Why was that?' The sergeant sounded positively friendly now.

'Well, I'm a nurse,' Pippa explained, 'and it was my first morning on Casualty—my escapade with the puppy made me horrendously late, which isn't the best way to start off, especially with a Casualty Officer who can be a bit of a pain in the neck.'

'No, miss,' agreed the sergeant, 'but surely it was your good deed for the day.'

'Quite, although I doubt whether he'd see it like that.'

Still smiling, she replaced the receiver, picked up her mug, took a large mouthful of wine, turned from the phone—then nearly choked as Richard Lawton stepped out of the dark passage.

CHAPTER FOUR

THE smile disappeared from Pippa's face and she stared at Dr Lawton dumbstruck as his gaze flickered from her tousled hair, tatty jeans and red shirt to the mug of wine in her hand. To add to her consternation, he was dressed in a navy blue towelling bathrobe with a white towel draped around his neck. His dark hair was wet and tiny rivulets of water ran down his face and neck, to disappear in the tangle of black hair that was just visible beneath his robe.

Then Pippa remembered something Sue Robinson had told her the previous day; that on the ground floor were two bathrooms that the residents of Maple House could use.

'Oh,' she said, finding her voice at last, 'you've been to the bathroom.' She could have bitten her tongue out the moment she'd made such an obviously silly statement.

Sardonically he raised one eyebrow, and she was struck afresh by how different he looked without those heavy-rimmed glasses.

'There wasn't a lot of point staying in my room. I had studying to do this evening, but I couldn't hear myself think, let alone work. Tell me, Miss Ward, do you intend having parties every night of the week? Or will all the excitement be over in one go?'

There was no disguising the sarcasm in his tone,

and Pippa, feeling a flush tinge her cheeks, was glad of the dimness of the light in the narrow passage. Taking a deep breath and trying hard to control her rising temper, she said, 'I'm sorry if you've been disturbed, Dr Lawton.' She almost called him *Mr* Lawton—after all, he'd called her Miss Ward instead of Nurse Ward—but she decided he would merely consider that childish, so instead she straightened her shoulders and, turning towards the stairs, added, 'I did try to keep the volume down, and, I assure you, it won't be happening every night of the week. It was simply a question of christening my new flat.'

He didn't answer, but as he followed her up the stairs his disapproval hung in the air between them like some tangible object. By the time they reached the landing Pippa was as embarrassed by his proximity as she was by the silence between them. But she couldn't find anything else to say that wouldn't sound silly or trite, and it was with a great sense of relief that they finally reached his flat.

She wondered if she should say something now; anything—goodnight even, and for one wild moment she felt hysteria rising, then she was saved from further humiliation as her flat door suddenly burst open and Claire and Tony appeared.

'Oh, there you are, Pippa,' said Claire. 'We're just off now. Super party. . .' She trailed off as she caught sight of Richard Lawton in his bathrobe. He had just inserted his key into the lock, but he glanced over his shoulder as she spoke. 'I think

the others will be going soon. . .' she added
lamely.

Afterwards Pippa didn't know how she'd had
the nerve, but as Dr Lawton turned to take his key
from the lock some wicked impulse goaded her
and she said, 'It's probably just as well you're all
going—Dr Lawton needs his sleep.'

With a look from his grey eyes that would freeze
molten lava he said quietly, 'That's right, I need all
the sleep I can get if I'm not to be a pain in the
neck the next day.'

When Pippa eventually got to bed that night she
slept only intermittently, waking almost every
hour to check her alarm clock in case she overslept
again. And while she was asleep her dreams were
strange; Claire with pieces of glass sticking out of
her legs and Tim Barnes wearing heavy horn-
rimmed spectacles and carrying a little girl in his
arms.

She was almost relieved when the alarm finally
went off, but she got out of bed feeling drained
and exhausted. Mechanically she prepared for
work, ate her toast and drank her coffee, and
found that when she was ready she was at least
half an hour too early.

She decided, however, that she might as well
set out for work, as she didn't want to take any
chances that morning on anything happening that
would make her late. The rest of the house seemed
very quiet as she left her flat, but as she crept past
Richard Lawton's door she heard faint sounds of
movement from inside, together with the sound of
classical music playing softly on the radio.

She gave a grim little smile as she slipped lightly

down the stairs. At least today she would be at work before him. The thought gave her some satisfaction as she stepped out into the icy morning and unlocked her car, saying the usual prayer that it would start. Luck or fate must have been on her side, for it started first time, and she sighed with relief as she drew out of the forecourt.

But her relief was soon replaced by anxiety as she approached the hospital. The thought of working in A and E for Dr Lawton had been bad enough, and that had been before last night's incident. Now, after making such a fool of herself, she was positively dreading the day ahead.

Whitford General was a vast sprawling complex of original Victorian red brick buildings interspersed with several modern blocks. It gave the impression that the architect had started out to try to blend them with the existing complex but had given up when it was necessary to add more and more.

That morning Pippa had the time to take a little more notice of her surroundings, and even found that she had a choice of spaces in the Casualty car park. As she got out of the car two porters called out to her from a passing milk-truck, and she smiled and waved back, recognising one of them from her days on the wards.

A sudden wave of nostalgia swept over her and she wished she were back in a normal ward instead of that charged-up atmosphere in Casualty. In fact, she wished she were anywhere rather than here. Then as she stood at the entrance to A and E an ambulance suddenly swung into the grounds, its blue light flashing eerily in the early-morning half-light.

With a slight screech of tyres it came to a halt in the bay before the large double doors, and, as she watched, several members of the night team appeared and with the ambulance attendant opened the doors. Two of them climbed into the back of the vehicle and seconds later a stretcher was lifted out. From the light above the doors Pippa caught a glimpse of a figure beneath a blue cellular blanket, a face strangely grey, half covered by an oxygen mask, and she heard snippets of talk from those in attendance. 'Get him into recovery. . .coronary unit. . .someone help his wife. . .'

A woman, her clothes untidy, her hair in rollers, a distraught expression on her drawn features, was helped from the back of the ambulance by an auxiliary nurse. Then they were gone, leaving Pippa standing on the spot. Suddenly she felt a tingle down her spine, a tingle of excitement that she was to be part of this unit where the drama of life and death was being played out hour after hour. Lifting her chin, she strode forward and through the double doors, ready to take whatever the day had to throw at her.

In complete contrast to the previous day Pippa was the first member of the day staff on the unit, but by the time she had changed Karen and Julie had arrived.

Karen laughed when she saw Pippa ready and waiting. 'I see you weren't taking any chances this morning,' she said.

Pippa pulled a face. 'No, I made a supreme effort.'

Karen began studying the duty roster, and at her next words Pippa's heart sank. 'Now, let's see,' she said, nibbling the end of her biro. 'Oh, yes, you're to go on A and E, Pippa—you'd better get over there now.'

With her heart thumping Pippa made her way across Reception, returning Gina's cheerful greeting, and pushed open the door of the A and E unit.

A charge nurse, Derek Henderson, met her, introduced himself and set her to work changing blankets and paper incontinence sheets. She worked steadily, then when she had finished she left the last of the cubicles and returned to the administration area. The first person she saw was Dr Lawton. He glanced up as she approached the desk and she stiffened, waiting for some sarcastic comment, but not by so much as the flicker of an eyelid did he indicate that he even knew her, let alone acknowledge what had happened the previous evening.

The unit seemed to be busy even at that early hour, and as Pippa hovered, wondering what she should do next, Derek Henderson appeared from a cubicle.

'Ah, Nurse Ward—good. I want you to go to the interview-room—it's down the corridor, second on the left. I'd like you to take Staff Nurse Jones's place. You'll find a Mrs Barrymore there. Her husband has just died and she'll be in shock. I want you to sit with her until her son arrives.'

Pippa nodded and was about to ask if there was

anything specific she should do, but Derek was gone, hurrying to answer a persistently ringing telephone.

She found the interview-room, tapped on the door and pushed it open, then she stopped in surprise. The woman from the ambulance, the rollers still in her hair, was sitting at the table, a cup of tea before her.

The staff nurse looked up at Pippa, but the woman was staring straight ahead.

'Have you come to sit with Mrs Barrymore?' asked the staff nurse.

Pippa nodded, and as Staff Nurse Jones stood up she took her place, then as the other girl quietly let herself out of the room Pippa glanced apprehensively at the silent woman. She was uncertain what she should do. Should she talk or remain silent? As she tried to reach a decision Mrs Barrymore suddenly spoke.

'He was worried about the pipes freezing,' she said without looking up. Pippa wondered if she'd even noticed that someone new had come into the room. 'He'd been outside to check them, he was so cold when he came back into the kitchen, and I put the kettle on to make some tea. He took his jacket off and hung it on the back of the door, then he went to the sink to wash his hands. . .that was all he did. . .and the next moment he was on the floor. . .' Her voice trailed off and she looked up in bewilderment at Pippa.

For a moment Pippa wondered if she should try and change the subject, but some instinct told her that Mrs Barrymore needed to talk about her husband, so quietly she leaned forward and, picking up the cup of hot tea, encouraged her to take it.

With the same bemused expression on her face the woman took the cup and saucer and began to sip the tea. 'We're going to Cheltenham later today to see his sister,' she said after a while. 'She's not been well lately, and Ernie and her have always been close—he worries about her, you see.' She took another sip. 'How long will I have to stay here?' she asked, and moved her eyes slowly in Pippa's direction as if seeing her for the first time.

'Until your son comes, Mrs Barrymore,' replied Pippa gently.

'David? Is he coming here?' The woman looked bewildered, then her hand started to shake and the cup rattled, slopping the remainder of the tea in the saucer. Pippa swiftly came to the rescue and returned the cup and saucer to the table. Mrs Barrymore put one shaking hand to her head and fingered the rollers.

'I must do my hair if David's coming,' she faltered.

Pippa glanced round and saw that Mrs Barrymore had had the foresight to grab her handbag before getting into the ambulance with her husband. 'Do you have a comb in your bag?' she asked.

The woman nodded vaguely, and Pippa retrieved the bag from the chair where it lay on top of her coat and waited patiently as Mrs Barrymore rummaged inside, then produced a red comb.

'Would you like me to do your hair for you, or

would you like me to get a mirror so that you can do it yourself?' asked Pippa.

Wordlessly Mrs Barrymore handed Pippa the comb, and within minutes Pippa had removed the rollers and put them on the table. Then carefully she combed through the thick grey hair in an attempt to get it into what she imagined was its usual style.

She had nearly finished when the door suddenly opened and a middle-aged man appeared in the company of Dr Lawton. The man looked white-faced with shock as he hurried to his mother's side. Pippa stood sympathetically aside as he embraced her, then she glanced at Dr Lawton.

At the sight of his expression, however, she froze. He was staring incredulously from her to the comb that she still held in her hand, and, even as she watched, his gaze travelled to the pink and blue rollers she had neatly lined up on the table. She opened her mouth to explain, but, before she could utter one word, he intervened. 'That will be all, thank you, Nurse Ward. I should like to speak to Mrs Barrymore now, if you've quite finished.'

Without a word she scooped up the rollers and dropped them into the open handbag along with the comb, and without another glance at either the woman, her son, or Dr Lawton she hurried from the interview-room.

Why, oh, why was it that Dr Lawton always seemed to misinterpret her actions? she asked herself as she made her way back to the administration area. She just didn't seem to be able to do anything right when he was around. She had no time for further speculation, however, for, on her return, the charge nurse immediately sent her to a cubicle to assist with a stomach wash-out.

It was the first time Pippa had witnessed one, and in spite of her curiosity she knew a moment's nausea herself as Julie Acland instructed her to hold the bucket for the patient to vomit.

The patient was a young woman who in normal circumstances would be strikingly beautiful, with her short black hair stylishly cut and an olive complexion. Now, however, she had quite obviously hit her lowest ebb. She had seemed only semi-conscious, but she fought against the tube that had been inserted into her mouth and down into her stomach.

'What's she taken?' asked Pippa, holding tightly to the bucket.

'We believe about thirty Paracetamol—washed down with about two-thirds of a bottle of vodka,' replied Julie as she poured more water into the large funnel connected to the rubber tubing.

The girl retched again and again, the smell in the small cubicle was almost overpowering, and Pippa wondered what it was that drove anyone to such extremes—was it emotional problems, or financial, or even something like failing one's exams? As the thought occurred to her, she made a promise to herself that she would seek Tim out later and encourage him to talk out his worries.

The first fluids in the bucket were saved for further analysis, but later, as the fluids ran clear, Julie stopped pouring water into the funnel and told Pippa to sit with the patient until the doctor came to see her.

She continued to hold the bucket as the girl still

retched violently from time to time. Once, in a
quiet period, she smoothed back the girl's damp
hair from her forehead.

'Don't worry,' she said softly, 'you'll be all right
now.'

At her words the girl turned sharply and with
one angry movement she dashed the bucket from
Pippa's hands. It bounced across the cubicle, shed-
ding its contents over the floor.

'I don't want to be all right!' hissed the girl.
'Why do you think I did it? Why can't any of you
understand?' With a gesture of pure misery she
turned her face to the wall, leaving Pippa to clear
up the mess.

She was only halfway through when Dr Scott
pulled back the curtains and summed up the
situation with a grim smile. Pippa felt a moment's
relief that this time it was Hannah Scott and not
Dr Lawton.

Dr Scott spoke to the girl, then requested a
blood test for a chemical assay before admitting
her to the ward for observation.

As Pippa took the wash-out equipment to the
sluice for cleaning she overheard Derek
Henderson telling Hannah Scott that the patient's
boyfriend had arrived. Hannah's reply was that
the boyfriend was in fact married and had left the
patient the previous night to return to his wife.

When Pippa returned to the office Derek asked
her to replenish the supplies in the larger of the
two treatment-rooms, which for a moment was
miraculously empty.

Carefully she made a list of all the items that
were running low in the glass-fronted cupboards,

then, taking a large plastic container, she went to the store cupboard and filled it with dressing packs, syringes, surgical gloves, absorbent gauze, crêpe bandages, surgical tape and all the other things that were in constant use in the treatment-room. Diligently she filled the shelves, and was just congratulating herself on a job well done when the doors behind her opened and she glanced over her shoulder. Her heart gave an involuntary jump as Dr Lawton strode into the room. He frowned when he saw her.

'What are you doing?' he asked.

Pippa swallowed, immediately on her guard in his presence, for it seemed that if there was anything to go wrong it would do so when he was around. 'I've just refilled the dressing cupboard,' she said, and her voice came out as little more than a breathless gasp.

'Good, there's an RTA on the way,' he said casually, as if road traffic accidents were of no more consequence than the arrival of the morning post.

Pippa turned to make her escape, but Richard Lawton had other ideas. 'You can stay and assist,' he said abruptly, and she felt her heart sink, wondering what she was going to have to face now. He walked towards the door as the sound of an approaching klaxon filled the air, then he paused and turned back.

'By the way, Nurse Ward, were you aware of the fact that Mrs Barrymore's husband had just died?' The question was casual, but there was a keen edge to his voice that for just a moment made

Pippa tremble. Then she straightened her shoulders and lifted her chin.

'Yes, Dr Lawton, I had been told.'

'I see—so did it not seem inappropriate to you to convert the interview-room into a hairdressing salon at that particular time?'

Pippa took a deep breath and tilted her chin a few degrees more. 'No, Dr Lawton, it did not,' she replied. 'In fact I believe that what I did may have helped the patient to a certain degree—at least, I hope it did.'

'And how did you come to that conclusion?' The grey eyes had narrowed watchfully.

'When Mrs Barrymore arrived with her husband she was still wearing her hair rollers—she was obviously in shock. . .'

'That was your diagnosis, was it, Nurse?'

'Yes. . .that is, I mean, she appeared to be very shocked. She wanted to talk about her husband, which I encouraged her to do, then she seemed worried that her son would shortly arrive and find her in her rollers. I think I merely helped her to feel better.'

'You think that was important, at that particular time, when a woman had just lost her husband, that she should be helped to look her best?'

'I don't know whether it was particularly important or not, I acted purely from instinct. . .an impulse, if you like. . .it just seemed to be the right thing to do at the time. . .' Miserably she trailed off and waited for a further reprimand or sarcasm, but instead, as the doors behind him were flung open and a trolley was wheeled in by an ambulanceman, he merely said, 'It seems to

me, Nurse Ward, you act on impulse rather a lot.'
Then he turned to the patient and Pippa was left
wondering whether she had in fact been repri-
manded or not.

The patient, a boy motor-cyclist of seventeen,
had been involved in an accident with a delivery
truck. He had sustained severe head injuries, was
unconscious and had multiple chest and leg
wounds. As the ambulance men, together with
Derek Henderson, lifted him on to the examination
couch and another nurse coped with the saline
drip that had been set up in the ambulance, Pippa
stole a look at Richard Lawton's face. She had been
about to move forward to try and help, but what
she saw halted her in her tracks.

Instead of his usual frown and slightly moody
expression she saw a look on his face that she had
never seen before. He was staring down at the
young lad, at his appalling injuries, and he looked
genuinely shocked. For a brief moment she wondered if he knew the boy, and it crossed her mind
that perhaps he was human after all, but then
professionalism took over, his features hardened
again and he moved forward, issuing directions at
the same time.

Pippa was instructed to remove the boy's clothing while Dr Lawton examined his eyes. She
hesitated, looking down at the torn and mangled
mess that had once been his legs, then gingerly
she leaned forward and began unbuckling his belt.

By this time the room was a hive of activity as
another team went to work on the driver of the
truck, who had been brought in with chest and
head injuries. As the boy's belt came undone and

fell apart Pippa unzipped his jeans, then, not knowing how she was going to remove them, concentrated for a moment on the buttons on his shirt.

Suddenly Dr Lawton swung round. 'What do you think you're doing?' he snapped.

'Removing. . .his clothes. . .'

'Not like that, girl, you'll take all day. Cut them off. . .quickly!'

Julie thrust a large pair of scissors into her hand, and with a gulp Pippa inserted a blade into one of the jagged tears in the boy's jeans and began to cut away the blood-stained material.

'I want X-rays, blood tests and cross-matching,' said Dr Lawton tersely as he continued with his examination.

The next hour passed in a blur to Pippa as first the boy, whose name turned out to be Terry, and then the truck driver, were taken to X-Ray, then admitted for emergency surgery. Throughout it all Pippa was intensely aware of Dr Lawton, aware of her increasing dislike for him, together with her helpless feeling of frustration that by now he must think her utterly stupid and incompetent.

CHAPTER FIVE

'I DETEST that man!' Angrily Pippa stirred her coffee and glared across the table at Claire. 'In fact,' she added when Claire didn't answer, 'I don't know how I'm going to stand working with him for ten weeks. I've a good mind to go to our nursing officer and ask if I can be moved.'

'Can we do that?' Claire looked up from her lunch, and momentarily Pippa was struck by how tired she looked.

'I don't know,' she admitted, and went on stirring her coffee, even though she didn't take sugar. Somehow she found the movement therapeutic.

'Is he really that bad?' Claire seemed to be showing interest now in what Pippa was saying, but until that point Pippa had suspected that her friend's mind had been elsewhere.

Pippa wrinkled her nose. 'He probably isn't, it's just that he puts me on edge, and when he's around I can't seem to do anything right.' She went on to tell Claire of the unfortunate incidents that had occurred and which had seemed to put her in a bad light in Richard Lawton's eyes. 'I really don't think I can stand much more of it,' she repeated as she finished.

Claire looked thoughtful. 'I don't see that asking to be moved would help. Wouldn't that put you in an even worse light, and with the nursing officer this time? I thought we nurses were supposed to be able to cope with anything.' She said it bitterly, causing Pippa to look up sharply.

'Is anything wrong, Claire?' she asked, concerned now by her friend's attitude.

'Wrong? No, why should there be?' Claire forced a smile, but it was too bright, and Pippa frowned.

'I don't know. . .you seem. . . I don't know, you just don't seem yourself somehow. . .' she trailed off lamely.

'I'm fine.' Claire finished her coffee and stood up. 'I must fly now, I'll see you later.' Then she was gone, leaving Pippa in a reflective mood to finish her lunch.

Claire had seemed so different in the last few days, not at all like the bundle of fun she usually was. First had come her strange statement about wondering if nursing really was for her, something she had never hinted at before, and now she was acting as if her mind was elsewhere. On top of that she didn't look particularly well.

Pippa sighed and stood up, her own problems temporarily forgotten as she concentrated on her friend. Her respite was shortlived, however, for as she entered the A and E unit for the afternoon shift the first thing she heard was Dr Lawton's voice, and he was asking where she was.

The afternoon was just as high-powered as the morning had been, and Pippa wondered if it was always like that on A and E. She broached the subject to Julie, while the older girl was showing her how to use the steriliser, which apparently had a mind of its own.

'I've never known a peaceful day on Cas,'

replied the older girl. 'Just when you think things may have gone quiet for a while you hear a klaxon and someone else is brought in.'

'Everything seems so well organised,' remarked Pippa.

'It has to be,' Julie replied. 'The casualty team is always highly trained and very efficient; it must be prepared for any emergency. Three years ago we had a dreadful plane crash when that jumbo jet came down on the school—do you remember?'

Pippa nodded. It had been in all the papers at the time and on every news bulletin, horrific scenes of the dead and critically injured.

'However did you cope with a disaster on that scale?'

'We have a special red alert procedure.' Julie glanced at her fob watch. 'Come on, I'll take you down to the red alert area and show you. Dr Lawton headed the team that day—he worked a forty-hour shift without a break; what he did was little short of miraculous.'

Pippa followed Julie through Reception, which was as crowded and noisy as ever, and down a corridor.

'I think I've got off to a bad start with Dr Lawton,' she said as they walked.

Julie smiled. 'In what way?'

'Well, for a start, I'm so clumsy when he's around. I do everything wrong—I'm sure he doesn't like me.'

'If it's any consolation, I was exactly the same when I came on this unit,' Julie told her, pulling a face. 'I think it's something to do with the sense of urgency. We all get so charged up with adrenalin, and in an effort to impress we do everything wrong.'

'You were the same?' Pippa threw her a surprised look. 'But you seem so efficient. I was watching you during that RTA, you knew exactly what to do, and even Dr Lawton was treating you with respect.'

They had reached a large set of double doors, and Julie stopped and laughed at Pippa's gloomy expression.

'You mustn't get the wrong impression of Dr Lawton just because he's a perfectionist—he's an incredibly clever doctor.'

'So everyone keeps telling me.' Pippa sniffed. 'I just wish he was a little more friendly. Is he always so abrupt?'

Julie frowned as she unlocked the doors and stood back for Pippa to enter the room. 'He's something of a loner, and, come to think of it, we never really see him outside the unit.'

'Doesn't he join in any of the social activities?'

'I've never seen him at anything, but that's not too unusual. From what I've heard he's well on the way to his consultancy, and the likes of them don't really mix with the likes of us.'

The room was vast, like some huge cavern, and it was packed with supplies and every conceivable piece of equipment that would be needed in any full-scale emergency. One area was stacked with blankets and stretchers, another with oxygen cylinders and packs of dressings.

'Practically everything in here was in use for the plane emergency,' said Julie, looking round. Her voice sounded strangely hollow in the vast room.

'And of course the floor area was cleared for the fatalities.'

'Didn't they go to the mortuary?' asked Pippa, knowing that was the usual procedure.

'Normally they would have done, but there were just too many of them. In the end, when the mortuary and the chapel were full, they started bringing them in here, and pretty soon this was full as well. Most of the plane's passengers were dead, and the badly injured, who were treated by the casualty team, were teachers and pupils from the school. As you can imagine, things became pretty chaotic, especially when relatives began arriving in their hundreds. The police were marvellous, but, as I said earlier, it was Dr Lawton who maintained absolute control throughout the whole alert.'

Pippa was silent, wondering if she'd misjudged Richard Lawton. From what she had heard so far it sounded as if he was regarded as some sort of a god amongst the people he worked with—but that still didn't give him the right to treat her the way he did.

The rest of the afternoon passed quickly almost without Pippa realising it, and before she knew it her shift was over and she was on her way home. She decided to spend a quiet evening catching up on a few jobs in her flat, but when she reached Maple House the first person she saw was Tim Barnes. He looked a good deal brighter than he had the previous day, and he smiled when he saw Pippa.

'Hi, there. Great party last night. Thanks—sorry I was such a pain.'

'That's all right, I quite understand,' replied Pippa as she leaned over the banisters to talk to him.

'I had a stinking headache this morning.' He smiled again, an infectious grin that lit up his whole face. 'Still, it serves me right, I suppose, for drinking all that red wine.'

'It was quite understandable under the circumstances,' said Pippa solemnly, pushing her hair back off her face. 'I honestly don't know what I'll do if I fail my finals.'

He shrugged. 'I know I've really got to buckle down to revision this time.' He had grown serious now and his blue eyes had darkened at the prospect of the daunting task ahead.

Pippa was silent for a moment, then impulsively she leaned forward. 'Listen, Tim. If it would be any help I'd be willing to give you a hand with some revision.'

His face brightened again. 'Would you? Would you really? I say, that's great—thanks a lot!'

'Just give me a shout when you're ready.' She smiled, and carried on up the stairs to her flat, while Tim stood in the hall watching her, then when she had nearly reached her landing he called after her.

'Pippa, how about this evening?'

'This evening?' She looked over the banisters at him.

'Yes, would that be OK? I'm in school tomorrow and I've got quite a bit to learn about renal failure.'

She hesitated for a moment as her vision of a quiet evening melted, then quickly she made up her mind. 'Yes, all right, Tim. Come up about eight o'clock.'

He arrived on the dot with two textbooks under his arm, stretched himself out on Pippa's sofa, then spent the next hour alternating between telling her how hard up he was and giving her a hilarious version of his experiences on the wards.

'Oh, Tim, you're impossible!' she gasped, wiping her eyes as he finished telling a story about a student who was asked to clean patients' false teeth and ended up collecting them all in the same bowl.

By the end of the evening very little revision had been done, for every time Pippa attempted to question him on his notes, he was reminded of another anecdote and would have her helpless with laughter.

'I'm not surprised you keep failing your finals,' she said sternly when at last she saw him to the door. 'You really will have to try harder, you know.'

He looked contrite for a moment and hung his head, his fair curls gleaming in the landing light. 'I know. . .but you will help me again, Pippa, won't you?' He looked anxious while she appeared to consider his appeal.

Then she smiled and nodded, 'Of course I will.'

He leaned forward, gently kissed the tip of her nose and said softly, 'Thank you—you know something? You're one hell of a girl.' Then he was gone, running lightly down the stairs, while she stood in the open doorway of her flat. She couldn't remember when she had laughed so much, and

her sides still ached. Shaking her head, she turned
to go back into her flat, and it was then that she
heard a faint click from the door across the landing. She paused and stared across at the door,
which quite obviously had just very quietly been
closed. Had Richard Lawton been listening to her
and Tim? Had he seen Tim kiss her?

She shrugged and closed her flat door. What if
he had? She certainly didn't care. Perhaps it would
do him good to realise what fun Tim was. It was a
pity he was so strait-laced about everything, she
thought as she prepared for bed. What he needed
was a good laugh, because for Pippa the evening
had acted as a wonderful tonic after the tensions
of the day.

The following morning as Pippa stepped outside, the air seemed damp and much milder, and
she was reminded of something her grandfather
used to say—three frosts, then rain. At least she
wouldn't have problems with the car, she thought
as she unlocked the door and slipped into the
driving seat.

It wouldn't start.

All her efforts, threats and cajoling were in vain
as the same grinding noise came time and time
again from the unobliging engine.

She was on the point of giving up when she saw
a motorbike slowly drive past the entrance of
Maple House. The rider, dressed in black leather
and a red crash helmet, appeared to be looking at
her.

Desperately she got out of the car and anxiously
glanced at her watch, wondering if she was too
late to catch a bus. As she locked her car she was

aware of a movement out of the corner of her eye and, looking up, she found that the motor-cyclist had got off his bike and had walked into the drive.

'Would you like a lift?' he asked. The visor of his helmet was pulled down, but there was something very familiar about the tall figure.

'Well. . . I. . .' She hesitated, immediately on her guard about accepting lifts from strangers but at the same time wondering if this rule only applied to strangers in cars.

'I have a crash helmet you can wear,' he went on, but still she dithered, then impatiently he lifted the visor and Pippa found herself staring up into the flint-grey eyes of Richard Lawton.

'Oh,' she gasped in astonishment, 'it's you!'

'Who did you think it was?' He gave an impatient sigh.

'I don't know. . . I didn't know you had a motorbike. . .'

He turned on his heel, and meekly she followed him out of the drive. Not only had she not known that he rode a motorbike, but she was amazed by the fact. It was the last thing she would have imagined of him. Most doctors at Whitford drove cars; the registrars and consultants the latest expensive models and the housemen and junior doctors souped-up sporty types.

The motorbike that stood propped against the kerb, however, wasn't exactly cheap, even Pippa with her inexperienced eye could see that. It was a huge monster with shining black paintwork and gleaming chrome. There were panniers either side of the rear wheel, the maker's name, BMW, was emblazoned on the petrol tank and it had more dials than her old Citroën.

Nervously she eyed the black leather pillion seat while Richard Lawton opened one of the panniers and produced the twin helmet of the one he was wearing. Without a word he handed it to her and watched as she fumbled to put it on.

'I've never been on a motorbike,' she muttered apologetically, convinced that she must appear a complete idiot.

'You've only to remember to hang on tightly,' he said, and for a moment his voice sounded more kindly. Then, moving closer, he reached out and picking up the ends of her scarf that she had flung casually around her neck, he crossed them over, covering her mouth. 'Can't have you getting cold,' he murmured.

She glanced up, still feeling foolish, then for a moment her eyes met his. She would have looked away again immediately, but something in his expression prevented her and she found herself staring at him, trying to read what she saw.

In the end it was he who looked away first. 'We'd better get a move on,' he said briskly, 'otherwise we'll both be late.'

Meekly she followed him and watched as he mounted the machine, then as he indicated for her to follow suit she took a deep breath and stepped forward. With one foot on the footrest she hesitated for a moment, then steadied herself by resting her hands on his shoulders before bringing her other leg over the bike, then gingerly she sat down.

He started the engine, and as the powerful

machine throbbed to life beneath her, he turned his head and shouted something, but his words were lost above the sound of the engine.

'I can't hear you,' Pippa shouted back.

'I said, all you have to do is to hold on,' he repeated.

She stared at his leather-clad back, then hesitantly placed her hands on either side of his waist, bracing herself as she waited for the bike to move. Instead he looked down at her hands.

'Don't you have any gloves?' he shouted.

'No!' she yelled back. She hadn't brought gloves because she didn't like wearing them for driving.

'Put your hands inside my jacket,' he ordered. 'You'll be frozen otherwise.'

She knew it was no use arguing, so, taking her hands from his waist, she slipped them up under his thick protective jacket and once again placed them around his waist. This time, however, there was only the thin fabric of his shirt between her hands and his body.

As the bike drew away she instinctively leaned forward and lowered her head. The smell of leather filled her senses, together with a faint scent of another kind, a deep musky smell, perhaps his aftershave, then as the bike gathered speed it was gone, whipped away by the wind.

There was very little traffic that morning and the powerful machine skimmed over the wet, deserted streets, eating up the miles. At first Pippa found herself gasping for breath, but she quickly got used to the sensation and was surprised by the unexpected feeling of elation as they gathered speed. She was glad he had told her to put her hands inside his jacket—they felt warm, partly from the coat's fleecy lining and partly from the heat from his hard muscular body.

When they neared the hospital Pippa felt a surge of disappointment. She wished the ride could go on. But she wondered what she was going to say to the others, especially Claire, after only the day before telling her just how much she detested Richard Lawton.

He drew into the car park and brought the machine to a halt, then after they had both dismounted, Pippa took off the borrowed crash helmet and handed it back to him. 'Thank you very much for the lift,' she said, shaking out her long hair.

'That's OK, can't have you being late again, can we?' he smiled. Pippa stared at him in amazement as she realised it was probably the first time she had seen him smile. It transformed his usually solemn expression, while the look in those flint-grey eyes had softened. She waited for him while he stowed the crash helmets into the panniers, then together they walked towards the main entrance.

'I didn't know it would be like that,' said Pippa as he opened the door and stood back for her to enter the unit, then as she brushed past him she once again caught that faint musky scent.

'Ah, but did you enjoy it?'

'Yes, I did. It's never exactly been one of my ambitions, but I must admit I found it quite exciting.'

He nodded as if he agreed with her statement,

then disappeared in the direction of the doctors' changing-rooms.

Pippa watched him go and with a little sigh she made her way to the nurses' room. Maybe she'd been too harsh in her judgement of him, she thought as she changed into her uniform and braided her hair. Maybe he wasn't so bad after all.

An hour later she had revised her opinion once again and reverted to her original impression. Along with his white coat Richard Lawton seemed to don his aloof air and abrupt manner, and it wasn't long before he was finding fault with the way Pippa worked.

Later, while she was checking some registration cards with Gina in Reception, she happened to mention that Dr Lawton had given her a lift that morning.

'On his motorbike?' Gina raised her eyebrows. 'You were brave—that's a real monster of a bike.'

'Actually I quite enjoyed it,' confided Pippa, who hadn't mentioned how she'd got to work that day to any of the nursing staff. 'I was rather surprised, though. I didn't expect him to have a motorbike, somehow.'

'He's ridden one for as long as I can remember,' replied Gina thoughtfully. 'I think he must be a bit of a fanatic; mind you, they cost a fortune, those machines, even more than some cars.'

Pippa nodded. 'I can imagine. Maybe he rides one to get through the traffic.'

Gina wrinkled her nose. 'I think there's more to it than that—as I said, I got the impression that he's a bit of a fanatic. I expect he belongs to one of those clubs.'

Pippa grinned. 'You mean like Hell's Angels?'

Gina clapped a hand over her mouth. 'Not quite. . .honestly, can you imagine it?' Both girls dissolved into fits of giggles, then struggled to bring themselves under control as a man lurched through the doors waving a bottle in one hand and shouting every known obscenity in the book.

'Oh, here we go again!' groaned Gina, the smile disappearing rapidly from her face. 'Get Derek, will you, Pippa? It looks as if I'll need some help with this one.'

Pippa found Derek in the office studying sets of X-rays with Dr Scott. She briefly explained what was happening, and he nodded, heading for Reception as he shouted for Mark, the casualty porter, to assist him. She barely had time to draw breath before Karen called her into a cubicle to hold a screaming child so that the doctor could stitch his lip.

The doctor, of course, was Dr Lawton, the child was hysterical and its mother distraught.

Pippa took the little boy on to her knee, but the tighter she held him the more he struggled. He had apparently put his teeth through his lower lip and gashed his forehead in a fall from a swing.

'You must hold him still, Nurse,' said Dr Lawton, and Pippa could hear the irritation in his voice, not with the child but with the mother, who wouldn't let him get on with the job, constantly bombarding him with questions.

In the end Dr Lawton strode from the cubicle, saying, 'I'll come back when everyone's calmed down.' And just for a second Pippa wondered if this was the same man who had told her to tuck her hands under his jacket so that they wouldn't get cold while they rode through the early morning together.

Eventually she persuaded the mother to go back to Reception and get herself a cup of tea, then quietly she talked to the toddler, calming him down to such an extent that when Dr Lawton finally returned he only had to contend with a quivering lip and a few spasmodic sobs.

Pippa kept busy throughout the day, but all the time at the back of her mind a question niggled; a question that asked what would happen when it was time to go home. Would Richard Lawton offer her another lift, or would he consider it didn't matter what time she got home and leave her to find some other way?

CHAPTER SIX

IT WASN'T until Pippa was halfway through Reception, buttoning her coat as she went, that Dr Lawton called out and asked her whether she wanted a lift home. She only hesitated for a moment, then accepted, and as she followed him to the car park she realised that she was actually looking forward to another ride on his motorbike.

This time, however, was vastly different from the early morning scene outside Maple House. Staff from the early shift were coming off duty by the score, and she found herself the object of several smiles and nudges, especially among her fellow students. Pippa contrived to keep a low profile, instinctively knowing that Dr Lawton would hate any form of speculation.

She needed no second bidding as to what to do this time, pushing her hair inside the crash helmet and mounting the pillion seat like a veteran. She even tucked her hands under his jacket without waiting for him to tell her to do so, but then as he turned his head she caught a glimpse of a smile on his face and wondered if she had been too forward.

As they drew out of the car park she saw Claire walking down one of the paths from the main hospital, and daringly she let go for a minute and raised one hand. Claire frowned, obviously not recognising her under the helmet, then as they

pulled away from the main entrance Pippa glanced
back and was amused to see Claire staring after
them, an astonished look on her face.

In spite of the fact that it was raining quite
heavily, the ride home was every bit as enjoyable
as the morning one had been, and by the time
they reached Maple House Pippa felt as if she had
been pillion-riding for years.

Dr Lawton pulled on to the forecourt for her to
dismount, then as she removed the helmet and
went to hand it to him she saw that he was staring
at her car.

'Have you got your car keys?' he asked.

She nodded and fumbled in her handbag, then
handed him her keys attached to a Save the
Whales key-ring.

'I'll park the bike, then I'll have a look and see if
I can find the trouble,' he said.

'That's very kind of you. . .but where do you
keep the bike?'

'I rent a garage in the lane at the back of the
house,' he replied, then, revving the engine, he
circled the big machine around the forecourt and
rode out of the entrance.

Pippa watched him, wondering why he couldn't
be as helpful at work, then with a little shrug she
turned and went into the house.

Tim Barnes was in conversation with someone
on the telephone, and, by the tone of his voice,
Pippa instinctively could tell it was a girl. When he
caught sight of her, however, he covered the
mouthpiece with his hand. 'Hi, Pippa, listen—I
must tell you, I've had the most brilliant idea as to
how I can save some money.'

'You have?' She laughed as she began climbing the stairs.

'Yes. I could move in with you. . .they say two can live as cheaply as one, don't they?'

She raised her eyebrows and would have made some suitably cryptic remark, but at that moment his attention was caught by the person on the other end of the line, who was probably thinking she'd been cut off, and he took his hand from the mouthpiece. 'Yes, my love, I'm still here,' he said, then, waving to Pippa, he mouthed. 'I'll be up later to discuss things.'

She laughed again and, shaking her head in disbelief, carried on up the stairs to her flat.

Once inside, the first thing she did, even before taking off her outdoor clothes, was to fill the kettle for a cup of tea, then by the time she had changed into a comfortable velour leisure suit the water had boiled. She brewed the tea, then, leaving it to stand, she raided the biscuit tin and found half a packet of chocolate digestives. Pippa found she was always incredibly hungry by about four o'clock when she was working an early shift.

She was just wondering what she could have for her supper that evening when she heard a knock on her door. 'Come in, Tim,' she called, smiling to herself. 'I've just made some tea, would you like some?' she added, hurrying through to the living area, then she stopped in surprise.

Richard Lawton was standing in the middle of the room. 'I'm afraid I'm not Tim,' he said, and for the first time ever she noticed a trace of awkwardness in his tone, 'but I came in anyway, and if the offer includes me I'd love a cup of tea.'

'Oh. . .oh, yes, of course,' she stammered, thrown into confusion by his sudden appearance. He was still wearing his black leather gear and his dark hair was flattened from the crash helmet. It gave him a strangely vulnerable look. Pippa gulped, then fled back to the kitchen.

She found a second mug and poured out some milk. 'Do you take sugar?' she called out.

'No, thanks,' he replied briefly.

A few minutes later, bearing two steaming mugs of tea and the plate of biscuits on a tray, she returned to find him staring at one of her posters. It was one that she'd chosen on impulse purely because it appealed; in sepia tones it depicted a little girl, possibly of the nineteen-twenties era, walking down a country lane dragging a teddy bear behind her.

Richard turned as she set the tray down on the coffee table, and her heart jumped as she saw that he had a familiar airmail envelope in his hand.

He held it out to her. 'This was on the hall table for you. You must have missed it when you came in.'

'Oh, thank you—yes, I was talking to Tim Barnes.' She reached out to take it, but he held on to it for a moment, staring down at it.

'Miss Philippa Ward—is that your name? Philippa?'

She nodded, and as he held out the envelope his eyes met hers. Crazily her heart seemed to skip a beat. 'I thought they called you Pippa,' he said softly.

'They do, but my real name is Philippa.' As she took the envelope from him, very briefly, her fingertips touched his and in sudden confusion she was forced to lower her gaze. 'My parents always call me Philippa. . .' She trailed off, embarrassed.

'It's a beautiful name; Pippa is pure sacrilege,' he said. 'I too shall call you Philippa.' He paused, then added, 'Off duty, of course.'

'Oh, of course,' she murmured, then, on another of her crazy impulses, she asked, 'Does that mean that I may call you Richard?'

He hesitated, only fractionally, but long enough for her to wonder how she'd had the nerve to ask, then mischievously she added, 'Only off duty, of course.'

He laughed then, and she was struck by how handsome he looked when he laughed and when his eyes weren't hidden behind his heavy-rimmed glasses. She indicated for him to sit down and he took off his leather jacket and sat in one of her armchairs while she curled up in a corner of the sofa.

He glanced at the envelope which she had put on the table beside the tray, promising herself a long, leisurely read when she was alone.

'Your parents are abroad.' It was a statement rather than a question.

'Yes, Australia for a month, visiting old friends. We lived there for six years when I was a child.'

'Will they be home for Christmas?' he asked.

'No,' she shook her head, 'not until the New Year. But I don't mind too much, because I'm on duty over Christmas.'

'You and me both,' he said, sipping his tea.

Pippa felt a pang as she realised they would be

working together over the holiday period, but she had difficulty interpreting her feelings. Suddenly she remembered why he was there, and she looked up sharply. 'Did you find out what was wrong with the car?' she asked, setting her mug down.

'Yes, it's your battery—it was flat.'

'Oh, dear, will I have to get a new one?' Mentally she was already counting the cost, but he shook his head.

'I don't think so—it probably only needs charging up.'

'I see.' She looked doubtful. 'The trouble is I don't have a battery charger.'

'Don't worry—I have,' he replied. 'I've already put it on charge for you, that's what I came up to tell you.'

'You have?' Her eyes widened in astonishment.

'Yes, it's in my garage. It should be OK by the morning.'

'Well, that's very kind of you.' Pippa floundered for something further to say. She was so surprised by his sudden burst of concern, which seemed rather out of character. 'I'm afraid I'm not very mechanically minded. I dread the car going wrong.'

'Ah, motorbikes are best,' he said, leaning back in the chair and stretching out his long legs before him.

'I always thought motorbikes were dangerous,' she said, trying not to look at his legs because the sight of his lean leather-clad thighs had stirred some emotion deep inside which she wasn't sure she could cope with.

'Correction,' he said. 'Motorbikes aren't dangerous, it's inexperienced people who think they
know how to ride them that are the problem.'

He fell silent, staring moodily into his mug, and
some half-forgotten thought stirred in Pippa's
mind.

She glanced tentatively at him. 'The boy they
brought into Casualty yesterday. . .the one in the
motorbike accident. . .?' She trailed off as she saw
his eyes darken.

'Yes, what about him?'

'Did you know him?'

'No, why?'

She shrugged. 'I don't know. I was watching
you when they brought him in and I thought you
recognised him.'

He was silent for a moment, then he sighed.
'No, I didn't recognise him.'

Pippa frowned. She could have sworn he'd
known the boy. He must have seen her puzzled
expression, for after a further moment of silence
he said abruptly, 'He reminded me of someone.'

She stared at him, waiting for him to continue,
but he seemed to be battling with some inner
emotion. 'Was it someone close to you?' she asked
quietly at last.

At first she didn't think he was going to reply,
then he said briefly, 'Yes, my brother.'

'Oh—oh, I see.' She was a little taken aback, but
when he offered no further explanation she asked,
'Have you heard how the boy is?'

'He died this afternoon.'

Her eyes widened, but his expression was
inscrutable.

'Oh, I'm sorry,' she said, not knowing what else to say.

Richard shrugged and replaced his mug on the tray. 'There was nothing to be done. His head injuries were too extensive, he was put straight on to a ventilator, but it was decided to switch it off late this afternoon.'

They were silent for a moment, then Pippa said slowly, 'I think that must be dreadful for the patient's family, knowing that he's alive. . .'

'No, Philippa,' he intervened swiftly, 'don't be under that illusion. When the brain is dead, as it was in Terry's case, the patient is dead. The support machine is merely acting as a pump, never forget that.'

She nodded, reassured by his words, and they were silent again, he apparently lost in his thoughts and she, while sorry that the young boy had died, also curiously elated by the fact that for the first time Richard had used her Christian name. She threw him a tentative glance. 'You said just now that the boy reminded you of your brother?' She sensed him stiffen at her question, and when he didn't reply she wished she hadn't spoken. 'Is he. . .your brother? Is he. . .?'

'Dead? Yes, Danny's dead. He too was killed in a motorbike accident.'

'Oh, I'm so sorry, I shouldn't have asked. . .'

'It's all right, it happened a long time ago.' He attempted a nonchalant shrug, but Pippa was not deceived and she knew he was still deeply affected. He glanced across at her. 'You know something? You're the first person here at Whitford that I've ever told about Danny.'

She felt her heart leap at his words, at the thought that he should have confided in her of all people, then they fell silent again while she battled to find something to say. In the end it was Richard who broke the silence; glancing round the room, he said, 'You seem to have settled in well here.'

'Oh, I have,' replied Pippa. 'It's so nice to be independent and not to have the warden breathing down my neck.'

'You were in the nurses' home before?'

She nodded. 'Yes. It was OK to start with, but— well, you know how it is.' She spread her hands.

'Yes, I agree there's nothing like your own place. . .'

'You can come and go as you please. . .'

'And have parties every night of the week if you want,' he concluded, then when he caught sight of her expression he smiled. 'Sorry if I was a bit of a pig, it's just that at the present time I have a lot of work to get through.'

'It's OK,' she smiled sheepishly. 'I do like a good time,' she admitted, 'but I don't make a habit of being a public nuisance. Have you been at Maple House very long?' she added as an afterthought.

He shook his head. 'No, not really. It's more of a stopgap than anything else. I'm moving into a new apartment shortly, but there's been a delay with the builders and I needed somewhere to live in a hurry.'

Pippa had just come to the conclusion that he really was quite human under that hard exterior when there came the sound of a knock and Tim stuck his head round the door.

'Hello, Pippa. Did you think I'd abandoned you,

my love?' From where he was standing Pippa
realised he couldn't see Richard sitting in the
winged armchair.

She opened her mouth to warn him, instinct
telling her he was about to make some inane
remark, but he was too quick for her. Shutting the
door behind him, he was already halfway across
the room when he said, 'Don't you think that was
a wonderful idea about us moving in together? I
knew the moment I set eyes on you that you were
the girl for me. . .' He must have seen the warning
look in her eyes then, for he trailed off, following
her gaze. As he caught sight of Richard Lawton,
however, he seemed totally unperturbed.

'Oh, hello there. Doc Lawton, isn't it?' He held
out his hand. 'I'm Tim Barnes, number one, downstairs—crazy, isn't it? Living in the same house
and we've never met.'

Richard stood up and nodded coolly at Tim,
then, turning to Pippa, he said quietly, 'I must be
going. Thank you for the tea. I'll replace the
battery first thing in the morning so you can use
the car for work.'

'Oh, thank you, thank you very much.' She
followed him to the door, suddenly overcome by a
feeling of desperation that something fragile had
somehow just been destroyed. This feeling was
confirmed when he turned in the doorway and
nodded briefly, and with a sinking feeling she
noticed that the bleak look was back in those grey
eyes.

She watched him cross the landing, then slowly
she closed the door and turned back into her flat.
Had he believed that Tim and she. . .that Tim was

going to move in with her? Or had he recognised it for the joke it was? Suddenly she felt like strangling Tim for being so stupid, then she caught sight of his contrite expression.

'Me and my big mouth!' he sighed. 'Do you think he believed what I said?'

Pippa shrugged and picked up the tray from the table. 'I can't imagine what he thought,' she said drily. 'But we might as well forget it; we can't do anything about it now.'

'No,' agreed Tim slowly as he followed her into the kitchen and watched as she rinsed the mugs. 'But he is your CO, isn't he?'

She nodded and pulled a face. 'He is, and don't I know it!'

Tim frowned. 'That's what I was meaning—from what you said before, it sounds as if life is difficult enough for you as it is without any ridiculous notions of mine messing things up.'

He was silent for a while and she knew he was watching her. When she made no further comment, he stepped forward and, putting his arms around her as she stood at the sink, he pressed his face into the hollow of her neck. 'On the other hand,' he murmured, apparently unaware of the fact that Pippa had stiffened involuntarily at his touch, 'maybe it wasn't such a ridiculous notion after all.'

As he tightened his grip she stepped back, treading heavily on his foot. 'I'm sorry, Tim, but no,' she said sharply, and struggled out of his grasp.

'Hey, take it easy!' He held up his hands in

surprise at the intensity of her reaction. 'I get the
message.'

They stared at each other for a moment; he, still
surprised and obviously hurt and she adamant but
also surprised by her reaction. Then she sagged
against the sink. 'Oh, Tim, I am sorry—it's
nothing against you, honestly. I guess I'm just not
into heavy relationships, and you caught me at a
bad moment.'

'Fair enough.'

'Still friends?' Anxiously she scanned his face.

'Of course.' He grinned, and she relaxed. 'Now,
do I get tea, or is that privilege reserved for
registrars?'

With a rueful smile Pippa filled the kettle again.

Later, however, after Tim had left and she was
alone she found herself wondering about her reaction to Tim's advances. She liked Tim, she liked
his personality and his sense of humour, there was
nothing physically objectionable about him, so
why had she acted the way she had? She had told
him she didn't want any heavy relationships, and,
while that was true to a point, she hadn't exactly
discouraged all advances that had been made to
her in her time at Whitford General. She had in
fact enjoyed several light-hearted friendships
which had simply fizzled out of their own accord.
So why had she resisted Tim so strongly?

Deep down she was uneasily forced to admit
that it had something to do with Richard, not
necessarily with him as a person but maybe more
to do with the fact that he had been in her flat
when Tim had made those misleading comments.

She hadn't wanted Richard to believe them, not only because they weren't true but because she hadn't wanted him to think badly of her. But why should that matter?

The deeper she probed the more confused she became. She decided that she had been angry with Tim not only for what he had said but for his bad timing. He had interrupted the first intelligent conversation she'd ever had with Richard Lawton. Until that moment she had always imagined that she had been portrayed in the worst possible light in his eyes; as a scatterbrained, clumsy student who acted on her impulses with scant regard for anyone else's feelings. While for her part she had never seen beyond the hard taskmaster, the stickler for etiquette and efficiency.

Then for that brief time, over shared mugs of tea, she had caught a glimpse of the man beneath the hard exterior. The glimpse had fascinated her and she had hankered to know more. The arrival of Tim had put paid to that, and she had a feeling that the moment of rapport and understanding between them had vanished forever.

Her fears were reinforced the following morning when in A and E he barely acknowledged her, treating her no differently from any other member of staff and leaving her wondering if she had dreamt that brief change in his attitude.

These feelings persisted for the next couple of weeks, during which time Pippa gradually settled down to life in Casualty, but couldn't get away from the fact that she still felt like a gauche schoolgirl whenever Dr Lawton was around. Away from the hospital she saw very little of him.

There were no more early-morning motorbike
rides, no chance encounters on the landing or the
stairs, and as Christmas preparations got under
way Pippa found herself wondering more and
more about her elusive neighbour. It finally
reached the point where she wondered if he was
deliberately avoiding her.

Then late one afternoon she was helping Gina
and Mark to set up the casualty Christmas tree and
was only half listening to their idle gossip when
she heard Richard's name mentioned. Immediately she paid attention.

'Apparently he was furious,' said Gina. 'Dr
Reynolds has been moved to another unit, and
goodness only knows what's happened to the
student.'

'What's this all about? Have I missed something?' asked Pippa.

'It was before you came on the unit,' explained
Mark. 'A junior houseman that we had here fancied his chances with a certain first-year student
nurse. I must admit she was rather tasty——'

'That's not the point,' broke in Gina. 'There are
rules about that sort of thing.'

'So what happened?' asked Pippa, looking from
one to the other.

'He was caught in bed with her at the nurses'
home in the middle of the afternoon.'

'Good grief! Who caught them?' Pippa
shuddered.

'The nursing officer,' replied Gina. 'The story
goes that she read the riot act to the student, then
reported the houseman to his superior, who just
happened to be Dr Lawton. He was furious that

the doctor had put his career on the line. To Dr Lawton that's just about the worst crime in the book, to jeopardise one's career.'

'That may be so, but it makes you wonder what our Dr Lawton gets up to over at Freelands.' Mark tapped the side of his nose.

'Do you reckon he has a woman?' Gina asked.

Mark grinned, then, glancing over his shoulder to make sure none of the senior staff were around, he said, 'What else would he keep going over to Freelands for?'

'Freelands?' Pippa frowned. 'What's at Freelands?' She knew from dealing with local patients that Freelands was an area to the north of the town consisting of several large housing estates.

'That's what we'd like to know,' said Gina as she began to pull yards and yards of coloured tinsel from a large cardboard box. 'Mark's granny lives up there, and Mark says he's seen Dr Lawton there several times recently. Oh, look at this tatty tinsel—you'd think they'd buy some new, wouldn't you?'

'No chance.' Mark shook his head, then, leaning over the reception counter towards the two girls, he added, 'It must be a woman. No one visits Freelands without a very good reason.'

Gina wrinkled her nose. 'It need not be a woman. Perhaps he visits a relative, some old uncle or sombody.'

'No, I'll bet it's a woman and she's probably married, that's why he keeps quiet about it.'

'Honestly, Mark, you really are the limit—you've got a one-track mind! I wouldn't think that sort of thing was Dr Lawton's scene at all.'

'Maybe not, but it doesn't alter the fact that I've seen him up there, does it?'

Gina turned to Pippa. 'He lives at Maple House, doesn't he?'

Pippa nodded.

'Do you see much of him, socially, I mean?' They were both looking at her with sudden interest now, and she swallowed.

'No,' she replied truthfully, 'I hardly ever see him.'

At that point she heard the sound of a klaxon and thankfully turned away. There was always a good deal of gossip and speculation on Casualty, just as there was on any of the other wards, but this particular piece of idle chatter had disturbed her and she was relieved to walk away.

The case that had just been brought in was a youngish woman with a heavy vaginal bleed. Derek Henderson asked Pippa to sit with the patient until the doctor could examine her.

Her name was Jenny Moreton, she was divorced from her husband and had three young children.

'I'm not pregnant again,' she said to Pippa. 'I know that's what they thought, but it's not a miscarriage.'

'How long have you been bleeding?' asked Pippa, noting how pale and drawn the woman looked.

'About eight days.'

'Is that normal for a period?'

'Oh, it isn't a period, it's the middle of the month,' Jenny replied. Suddenly she looked frightened and threw Pippa an anxious glance. Pippa didn't allow herself to show any reaction and instead began asking about the woman's children. Immediately she produced photographs from her handbag and they spent the next ten minutes talking about the youngsters.

By the time Dr Lawton arrived Jenny was much more relaxed than when she had first arrived. He closed the curtains behind him and indicated for Pippa to stay, then he proceeded to question the patient about her periods. She gave him the same answers that she'd given to Pippa, and once again Pippa saw the flicker of fear in her eyes.

'When did you last have a smear?'

The woman avoided his gaze. 'I'm not sure. . .about two years ago, I think.'

'And was it negative?'

'They said,' she sighed, 'they said I had to have another one in about a year's time.'

'And why haven't you?' He asked the question gently, casually almost, as if it were of little consequence, and when the woman replied that she hadn't had the time, what with the children and her job, he didn't by so much as the flicker of an eyelid indicate that he might be annoyed. Then he examined her and gently but firmly told her that he was admitting her to the gynaecological unit for further investigation.

Julie Acland arrived to make arrangements regarding the woman's children with Social Services, and Pippa followed Dr Lawton into the office.

'What do you think's wrong with her?' she asked as he peeled off his surgical gloves.

He raised his eyebrows. 'It could be one of a

number of things; it could be fibroids or a particularly heavy period, or. . .' he paused '. . .or what do you think, Nurse Ward?'

She hesitated. 'It could be cervical cancer, couldn't it?'

'Yes, it could be, quite easily, especially with the history she gave us, just as it could quite easily have been prevented if only she'd had her follow-up smear.'

'Do you think she knew?' asked Pippa quietly.

'What do you think?'

She nodded. 'Yes, I think she knew. She was very frightened.'

'You did well with her, Nurse Ward,' he said as he turned to leave the office.

'I did?' Her eyes opened wide in disbelief.

'Yes. Apparently she was practically hysterical in the ambulance. You seem to have the knack of calming people down. Well done!' He strode from the room, leaving Pippa staring after him in astonishment. It was the first time she'd ever heard any word of praise from him, and she felt a warm glow deep inside.

CHAPTER SEVEN

PIPPA mentioned the fact that at last she seemed to have done some right in Dr Lawton's eyes later that evening when she joined Claire, Mandy and some of the other students in the hospital social club for a drink.

'I gathered he was being more friendly towards you,' remarked Claire.

Pippa frowned. 'What do you mean?'

'Well, didn't I see you on the back of his motorbike?'

'Oh, that!' Pippa tried to sound casual but was annoyed that a flush had touched her cheeks. 'That was ages ago, and it was only the once, when my car wouldn't start.'

Mandy grinned. 'You were honoured. You never know, Pippa, if you play your cards right. . .' She winked.

'Don't be so silly!' Pippa retorted, and it came out sharper than she had intended. 'There's nothing like that.'

'All right, keep your hair on! I was only joking— and besides, it's about time you found someone. It's months since you went out with anyone.'

Pippa shrugged. 'There's no one I'm interested in at the moment,' she said.

'That isn't what I heard,' said Claire, standing up and draining her glass.

'What do you mean?' Pippa stared up at her indignantly.

'Well, a little bird told me that Tim Barnes has been spending quite a bit of time in a certain student nurse's flat in the evenings.'

'Oh, Tim,' Pippa waved her hand in a dismissive gesture. 'I've been helping him with his revision, that's all—honestly,' she added when the other two girls laughed knowingly.

'Well, I've heard it called some things. . .' Mandy began, then shrugged her shoulders and fell silent as Claire glanced at her watch.

'I'll have to fly, I'm supposed to be meeting Tony in ten minutes. 'Bye for now, see you tomorrow.' She was gone in a swirl of her navy cape, leaving the other two girls to finish their drinks.

'Is Claire all right, do you think?' asked Mandy after a while.

'Why do you ask?' Carefully Pippa set her glass down.

'I'm not sure really, but she seems to have changed recently.'

'I'm glad you've noticed it as well, I thought it was just me,' said Pippa, relieved to hear someone else voice concern over Claire.

'So what do you think it is? Do you think it's anything to do with the job, or is it Tony?'

Pippa slowly shook her head. 'I'm not certain, but just recently she did say that she'd had some doubts about nursing. I did wonder if she was thinking of giving up.'

'It would be a shame after getting so far,' mused Mandy. 'But on the other hand, as we all know, if the dedication goes there's no earthly point in going on. Is she going home for Christmas?'

'Yes.'

'Well, maybe that will be "make your mind up time" on whatever the problem is. Talking of Christmas, you're on duty, aren't you, Pippa?'

Pippa nodded. 'Yes, Christmas Eve and Christmas Day, but I'm off on Boxing Day. I wonder if Cas is as chaotic at Christmas or whether people are too busy to injure themselves?'

'How are you getting on in Cas? Do you like it?' Mandy looked curiously at her friend. She still had her spell to do in Casualty and was eager to know what was in store for her.

'I think I do,' Pippa answered slowly, reflecting on the past three weeks. 'It's very exciting, I've never known anything like the adrenalin surge you get while you're waiting for an ambulance to arrive, then you hear the klaxon and see the blue light and you have to mentally prepare yourself for any eventuality. Then the team swing into action and you either go with them, or, on a good day, you're pushed aside, and on a bad one, trampled underfoot.'

'It sounds tremendous—so why are you unsure whether you like it or not?'

Pippa hesitated. 'I think it's because I never see what happens to a patient. When you're on the wards you see people come in, have their operation or treatment, hopefully recover and go home. On Cas your only involvement is that initial assessment period.'

'A vital one, nevertheless,' observed Mandy.

'Oh, yes, don't get me wrong, I would never

underestimate the tremendous job they do. I just find it difficult not to be able to see the outcome of the actions. I've never been in such a highly organised or efficient place in my life,' Pippa added thoughtfully, 'and most of that's down to the CO.'

Mandy threw her a glance. 'All joking aside, are you getting on better with him now?'

'Well, as I said earlier, he actually gave me some praise today, so things must be looking up. Having said that, tomorrow he'll probably bawl me out for doing something wrong.'

'He's certainly rather dishy—does he ever come in here?' Mandy set her glass down and peered around the dim interior of the club.

'I don't think so. I've never seen him in here. I wouldn't think it's his scene somehow. He appears to spend most of his time working or studying.'

'You mean there's no woman?' Mandy wrinkled her nose.

Pippa hesitated, suddenly reluctant to pass on the gossip she'd overheard in Reception that day. 'No,' she said at last, 'I don't believe there is.'

Later, however, as she drove home she found herself thinking about what Mark had said, and wondered if there was any truth in what he had implied about Richard visiting a woman at Freelands.

Casualty continued to be busy during the run-up to the festive season, and the following day was no exception. Patients packed the reception area waiting to be seen with everything from a child with a broken wrist to an elderly lady brought in suffering from hypothermia.

The weather had turned very cold again, with a north wind and ice on the puddles in the car park. Pippa still had hopes of a white Christmas, and mentioned the fact to Sister Gould as the two of them watched one of the hospital electricians turn on the lights on the casualty Christmas tree.

'It sounds romantic,' commented Rose Gould, 'but, believe me, it would increase our workload. The accident rate soars with the arrival of snow.'

'Yes, I suppose it would.' Pippa glanced round at the waiting patients, their ailments practically forgotten as they watched the ceremony of the lights. 'Although it's hard to imagine being any busier than we are now.'

'Oh, we can be. You just wait, my girl!' Sister laughed. 'To coin a phrase, "you ain't seen nothin' yet"!'

At that moment a noisy commotion outside Casualty claimed everyone's attention, and within seconds they were invaded by what appeared to be an entire rugby team.

Sister Gould quickly got the situation under control when it transpired that the team were visiting Whitford from their native Wales to play a local side in a charity match that afternoon. One of their number had fallen down the steps of their coach and apparently dislocated his shoulder. The group were adamant that they had to accompany their team-mate, who should be seen immediately, but they were finally persuaded to sit in Reception and take their turn.

But what Sister Gould hadn't bargained for was their noisy rendition of their traditional rugby songs together with a variety of seasonal carols.

This, along with their obvious appreciation of the female members of staff, provided entertainment for patients and staff alike.

Even Dr Lawton saw the amusing side of the situation, much to Pippa's amazement, but she later suspected him of queue-jumping to restore peace to the unit.

'Well, it's made my morning, anyway,' said Gina with a grin as Pippa passed the desk on her way to A and E.

'Yes, it's nice to have a bit of light relief,' agreed Pippa. 'Oh, look, here they come—it looks as if the fun's over.'

Escorting their colleague in their midst, the group were making their farewells, professing undying love for the angels in uniform and blowing kisses to other female patients. Then they were gone, and while the staff were still laughing, weak with relief at the sudden peace, an ambulance screamed to a halt, its blue light flashing. Pippa jumped and automatically ran to the double doors with Karen and Derek Henderson.

As the driver literally fell out of his seat, Derek said, 'It's a child, a three-year-old, sliding on the ice on a garden pond when it gave way.'

Pippa felt her heart leap, then as the vehicle's doors were flung back the attendant was down the steps in a flash, a blue bundle in his arms. A couple followed, a young woman verging on the hysterical and a man, ashen-faced and silent.

For the next half-hour Pippa hovered on the edge of the group in the resuscitation-room as the team fought for the toddler's life. The team comprised Dr Lawton, Hannah Scott, Derek Henderson and Karen, and, as they worked fran-

tically, one of them would occasionally ask Pippa
to fetch some piece of equipment or assist in some
small way.

Two images became imprinted on Pippa's mind,
and she was to remember them for days afterwards. One was the grim, dedicated expression of
Richard Lawton as he struggled desperately to
instil life into the tiny form on the table, and the
other was the face of the child himself—the trans-
lucent skin, blue-tinged beneath a crop of fair curls
and the thick dark lashes, motionless on his
cheeks.

Silently Pippa found she was praying, willing
the team to succeed so that someone, anyone,
could leave the room and go to the distraught
parents and tell them their world hadn't come to
an end.

Then she caught a glance between Richard
and Hannah, a glance that spoke volumes before
Richard shook his head.

'I'm sorry,' he said. 'There's no point going on,
we can't do any more for the little lad.'

Wildly Pippa stared from one to the other.
Whatever did they mean, they couldn't do any
more? Of course they could! They had to, they had
to keep trying.

Richard had turned to Rose Gould, who had
silently come into the room. 'Can we leave things
to you now, Rose?' he said quietly. 'I'll speak to
the parents, of course.'

'But. . .but you can't just give up!' Someone had
shouted out, and vaguely Pippa recognised the
voice as hers. But it was as if she were viewing the
scene from a distance. Dimly she was aware that

everyone had turned towards her, but nothing could have stopped her now.

'You mustn't. . .you mustn't give up!' she cried. 'He may still be alive!' Her wild gaze met Richard's and with a sigh he looked at Sister Gould.

'Sister, can you control your staff a little better, please? Otherwise, might I suggest that Nurse Ward goes off duty for a while?'

'Leave her to me,' said Sister Gould firmly, then as Richard and Hannah left the room she whispered something to Karen, who also disappeared, leaving her alone with Pippa.

'Come along, Pippa,' she said, 'we have work to do.' Tenderly she looked down at the child.

'What do you mean?' There was a note of hysteria in Pippa's voice.

'We have to get this little lad ready for his parents to see him. . .'

'But. . .'

'No buts, Pippa, it has to be done. It's all part of nursing, you know.'

'How did they know when to stop?' whispered Pippa, willing herself to look at the child, who appeared to be sleeping peacefully.

'He was dead, Pippa. There was no sign of a pulse, his breathing had stopped. They did all they could, you have to believe that—he'd drowned. Ah, here's Karen.' Sister Gould glanced up as Karen appeared again. She was carrying a small pair of neatly folded pyjamas, and as she shook them out Pippa saw they were covered with Paddington Bear designs. She gulped and realised a huge lump had risen in her throat, then she took a deep breath and had to force herself to watch as the two older nurses dressed the little boy in the pyjamas Karen had brought from the children's ward.

'Now, we'll just comb his hair,' said Rose. 'Then, Karen, perhaps you'd bring his parents in.'

At that point Pippa fled, and with tears streaming down her cheeks she dashed through Reception, ignoring Gina's startled look, and, bursting into the staff-room, slammed the door shut behind her.

For a moment she leaned against the closed door, struggling for control, then as a great sob threatened to choke her she moved across the room to the window.

Leaning on the sill, she stared out at the obstetrics wing opposite. It was more than likely that the little boy had been born in that wing. Now he was dead, and the tiny body would soon be taken to the mortuary at the rear of the hospital.

So intense were her anguished emotions that Pippa didn't hear the door open behind her, and it wasn't until she felt strong arms go round her that she jumped, and, turning, found Richard behind her.

For a moment she simply stared at him, her cheeks still wet, her eyes swimming with tears.

'I'm sorry, Philippa,' he murmured, and there was an infinite tenderness in his tone she had never heard before. 'I shouldn't have been so hard on you,' he added, and, as she sagged against him and her face crumpled, he tightened his grip, holding her against his body. 'Go on, have a good cry, if that's what you want, and get it out of your system.'

For a while she sobbed helplessly, drenching the front of his white coat, then as the storm subsided she said between gasps, 'I know I made a fool of myself, but I couldn't accept that there was no more to be done.'

'I know, I know. . . I feel it myself frequently; that powerless emotion that tells you you no longer have control.'

'But you seem so able to accept these things, you seem so. . .so. . .' Desperately she searched for the right word.

'So hard?' he said quietly, and, still holding her against him, he took his handkerchief from his pocket and gently wiped her face. 'Yes, I expect I appear hard, I expect we all do, but it's a shell, Philippa, a shell we all have to develop if we're to survive in this profession. Because, underneath, we hurt, don't make any mistake about that. If we're to succeed as doctors or nurses, that shell has to encase a deep core of compassion. Without that we might as well not bother.'

'Sometimes I wonder if I've made a mistake,' said Pippa slowly, taking the proffered hankie and blowing her nose. 'Sometimes I don't think I'll ever acquire what it takes to be a good nurse.'

'I'm not sure it's something that can be acquired,' he replied thoughtfully. 'I think it's rather something you're born with.'

'A gift, you mean?' Her tears under control now, she looked up into his face. He was staring out of the window and there was a faraway look in his grey eyes, but still he continued to hold her.

'Yes,' he agreed at last, 'a gift. A gift for healing and caring.'

For a moment Pippa remained silent, aware of his heartbeat beneath his white coat, and once again she caught that musky aroma she'd noticed the last time she'd been close to him.

Suddenly he seemed to realise he still had his arms around her, and he stepped back.

Pippa sighed. For some inexplicable reason she had wanted him to stay where he was with his arms around her, holding her against his chest.

'Did you speak to the boy's parents?' she asked, wanting to prolong this unaccustomed intimacy between them, for she knew that the minute they stepped beyond the staff-room door the old formalities would be back.

He nodded, and his smile was replaced by a grim expression. 'I did, and I think that has to be the hardest task of all.'

'How did it happen? Someone said something about a garden pond.' Suddenly Pippa felt anger surge up inside her. 'Why didn't they watch him? Why wasn't the pond covered, with a toddler around?'

'Apparently it was a neighbour's pond.' Richard sighed, but he didn't seem angry. 'The mother was visiting and it seems the little lad wandered outside. They said he'd been watching older boys sliding on puddles on the supermarket car park. He obviously thought he could do the same, but of course the ice was very thin. There'll naturally be an inquest, so no doubt we'll know more then, although I doubt very much whether there'll be any more to hear. Very often the simplest of circumstances surround these tragedies. Now,

Philippa,' he said gently, 'do you feel like returning to the unit?'

She swallowed and nodded. 'Yes, just give me a minute to tidy myself up—and thank you, Richard, for being so kind.'

He smiled. 'We are quite human, you know. . .underneath.' Then he was gone, and she was left staring at the closed door and wondering if she'd dreamt what had just happened, then she looked down, and the handkerchief in her hands told her otherwise.

The atmosphere on the unit when Pippa returned was very subdued, and as the day went on she realised that what Richard had said was quite right. The staff were affected by these traumatic events, but what she had thought of as their hardness, she now understood, was their way of coping, if they were to keep going.

In the end it was Hannah Scott who attempted to raise everyone's spirits by reminding them of the party she was holding the following night.

'I hope you'll all come,' she said, looking round at the team, most of whom were enjoying a rare break in the staff-room.

'You won't get us all in your little flat,' said Julie with a laugh.

'Ah, but that's what I haven't told you,' said Hannah, flicking back her shoulder-length blonde hair. 'I'm not holding it at the flat.' She paused for effect and everyone looked up with sudden interest. She smiled and glanced round at the expectant faces. 'My parents are away, and they said I could use the house.'

A ripple of interest ran round the room, and

Pippa remembered that she'd heard somewhere that Hannah's father was a wealthy barrister and the family home was a beautiful old farmhouse.

'I hope they know what they're letting themselves in for,' said Derek sadly, shaking his head.

In the midst of the laughter that followed his remark, the door opened and Richard came into the room.

Pippa felt her heart jump at his sudden appearance. She hadn't seen him since he had comforted her earlier in the day.

'Oh, here's Richard.' Hannah stood up. 'I don't suppose there's much point my trying to persuade you to come to my party tomorrow night. I know parties aren't usually your scene.'

He frowned. 'Tomorrow night?' He hesitated. 'I won't make any promises, because I have an appointment over at Freelands—it just depends what time I get away.'

'Sounds as if this party might go on all night,' said Mark as a buzzer sounded on the wall, warning them of an imminent casualty.

They all began to file from the room, and as she reached the door Hannah paused and stood aside for Pippa. 'You're included in the invitation as well, Pippa,' she said.

'Oh, am I?' Pippa suddenly felt pleased, for she'd wondered if the invitation had only been for permanent members of the team and not extended to students.

'Of course,' replied Hannah firmly. 'You're one of us now.'

Pippa felt a glow spread through her and, suddenly embarrassed, she glanced over her shoulder, to find Richard watching her, having quite obviously heard what Hannah had said.

Later that evening, in the privacy of her flat, Pippa found herself going over and over the events of the day in her mind. The disturbing images of the child and the surrounding drama kept recurring, but there had been another aspect of the day's events that she also found difficult to come to terms with.

When she had first met Richard Lawton she had taken an instant dislike to him. This feeling had continued as she had always seemed to feel gauche and unsure of herself whenever she was in his presence. Then had come the incident when he had given her a lift on his motorbike, and at that time she had felt that maybe they had established a better relationship.

After that, however, she had had the distinct impression that he'd been avoiding her, and when they had come into contact at work it had been as before, with him finding fault with almost everything she did. The events of the past day, however, had changed things yet again, and she found herself confused by the strength of her emotions whenever she thought about the kindness he had shown her.

Her friends had joked that there might be more to her relationship with the registrar, and she had dismissed their notions with contempt, but now her confusion prevented her from analysing her emotions.

She stepped out of the shower, pulled on a towelling robe and began to dry her long hair. It was ludicrous to think there might be anything between them—they were worlds apart; he a successful registrar on his way to the top of his profession and at least ten years older than her, and she a humble student nurse not yet twenty-one.

Besides, she thought, pulling a face at her reflection in the mirror, he didn't even like her, and, as Mark had hinted, there probably was a woman somewhere in the background, a fact almost confirmed by Richard himself when he had said he had an appointment in Freelands the following evening.

Suddenly she heard a knock on the door of her flat, and because she was thinking of Richard, she stiffened, thinking it might be him. Tightening the belt of her robe, she hurried across the living-room and pulled open the door.

CHAPTER EIGHT

CLAIRE stood on the landing, her face red and her eyes swollen from crying. Pippa stared at her friend in astonishment, and it was Claire who spoke first.

'I need someone to talk to,' she said, and her voice was barely more than a whisper.

Taking her wrist, Pippa pulled her gently but firmly into the flat and closed the door. It was another bitterly cold night and Claire looked chilled to the bone, her small features pinched and blue.

Pippa sat her down on the sofa, and, in spite of the fact that the central heating was on, turned on the gas fire. It wasn't until she'd made two steaming mugs of coffee and both girls were ensconced on the sofa that she attempted to find out what was wrong.

By then Claire seemed unable to know where to start, and Pippa gently tried to question her.

'Is it Tony?' she asked, watching the other girl's face carefully.

Claire shook her head.

'Not getting more involved than you'd intended?'

Again Claire shook her head, and Pippa felt a fleeting sense of relief, for just for a moment, when she'd opened the door, it had crossed her mind that her friend might be pregnant.

'No, it isn't Tony,' said Claire. 'In fact he's been wonderful—I don't know what I'd have done without him. But now I feel he's too close to the problem, and I need some advice, because I just don't know what to do.'

As she was speaking, Pippa's eyes had narrowed as she thought she caught a glimpse of the problem.

'Claire, is it nursing that's the trouble?' she asked.

'Nursing?' Claire looked up, but there was a blank look in her blue eyes.

'Yes. A little while ago you said you were beginning to wonder if you'd made a mistake and whether or not nursing really was for you. If that's your problem, then I know exactly what you mean. I've had a dreadful day today in Casualty and at one point I was ready to chuck the whole thing in, I can tell you. But now. . .now that I've had time to think, I realise that we're bound to feel like that sometimes——'

'It isn't that,' interrupted Claire dully.

'It isn't? But I thought. . .you said. . .' Pippa looked bewildered.

Claire gave a deep sigh and set her mug down on the coffee-table. 'I know that's what I said, but I guess I was only trying to find excuses.'

'Excuses for what?'

'Excuses for giving up my training.'

'But I don't understand. . .why should you need excuses?' Pippa was more confused than ever now. 'Do you want to give up your training?'

Claire shook her head. 'No, I want to qualify more than anything else in the world.'

'Then why? Claire, for goodness' sake, you're not making any sense! Whatever's happened to make you feel like this?'

'My mother's left my father.' Claire said it without any emotion, as if she were stating the price of a loaf of bread, as if all feeling had been wrung out of her.

'What?' Pippa stared at her in amazement, hardly able to take in what she had heard. She had met Claire's parents on several occasions, the last being less than a year ago when they had celebrated their silver wedding.

'She's left with Dad's best friend. Dad's absolutely devastated.' Claire looked up, and her eyes were suspiciously bright again. 'I just can't believe it, Pippa!'

'Oh, Claire, I'm so sorry.' Pippa leaned across the sofa and put a comforting arm around her friend. She knew what a close family the Frenches had been, and she guessed this would destroy them. 'How long have you known about this?' she asked after a while.

'About three months.'

'And you've kept it to yourself all this time?'

'I kept hoping it wasn't true, that she wouldn't go. Then when she did, I hoped she'd come back, but now there doesn't seem much chance of that.'

They were silent for a while, each busy with her own thoughts, then gently Pippa said, 'Claire, I can only imagine what you and your dad must be going through, but I'm not sure that I understand how it's connected with your training.'

Claire was staring at the realistic embers on the gas fire and she didn't answer immediately, then slowly, without looking at Pippa, she said, 'I feel I should go home.'

'But why? Your dad always seemed so proud of the fact that you were training. I'm sure he wouldn't want you to give it up now. . .in spite of what's happened.'

'You don't understand. If it was only me it wouldn't be so much of a problem, although, as I said, Dad is devastated and I feel he needs all the support he can get, but the real problem is my brothers. They're still quite young, and I don't know how Dad's going to cope on his own.'

Pippa suddenly felt a stab of anger for the selfishness of the woman whom she hardly knew, but who had caused so much chaos in the lives of her children. When Claire lapsed into silence again Pippa took a deep breath. 'You know, Claire, I think you may be jumping to conclusions. I'm sure that once your father sorts himself out the last thing he'd want is for you to give up your career. You'll probably find he'll get someone in to help with the boys.'

'That's not the same. . .it wouldn't be family.'

'Maybe not, but I still say he wouldn't want you to give up nursing.' Pippa paused, then she said, 'Listen, Claire, you're going home for Christmas, aren't you?'

The other girl nodded with a look that clearly implied it wouldn't be much of a Christmas.

'Well, you must discuss this with your father. . .now, when do you go?'

'The day after tomorrow.'

'In that case first thing tomorrow you must go

and see our tutor and tell her what you've told me.'

Claire nodded. 'Tony said I should do that.'

'What does he think about it?' asked Pippa.

Claire gave a wan smile. 'He says exactly the same as you.'

'Well, there you are, then, we can't both be wrong,' said Pippa firmly.

There was no sign of Richard Lawton the following morning when Pippa left Maple House, but she found that for the first time since starting on Casualty she was actually looking forward to going to work. She tried to convince herself that this new frame of mind was because she was settling down and getting used to what was expected of her and had nothing at all to do with the CO.

When she arrived, however, she found they were short-staffed, with two nurses off sick.

'The usual spate of absenteeism with the festive season coming up,' said Karen unsympathetically, then, glancing at the duty rota, she added, 'You'd better go over to A and E again this morning, Pippa, and give them a hand, then later if things quieten down you can come back here and help with dressings.'

Pippa felt her heart leap with pleasure and she hurried across Reception to A and E.

She was met by Derek Henderson. 'Are you with us this morning, Pippa?' He looked a bit harassed, which was unusual for him, and when Pippa said that Karen had sent her to help she was surprised and pleased when he replied, 'Thank goodness for that, we need all the sensible help we can get as we're so short-staffed.' He glanced up at the large blackboard above the desk. 'Right, first I want you to accompany a patient to X-Ray. He's an elderly man and he appears to have fractured his femur. He's been given pain-killing injections, but he's in need of reassurance.'

When Pippa later returned to the office with the X-ray films she watched as Dr Scott transferred them to a lighted screen and carefully followed the lines of the patient's bones with the point of her pen. The film confirmed the fracture, and Derek rang through to Orthopaedics for a bed for the patient. As Pippa watched while he spoke to the surgical registrar she became aware that there was a different atmosphere on the unit that morning. Even she was feeling edgy, but she wasn't sure why. She glanced round the office to the treatment-room beyond, then it dawned on her what was wrong; she hadn't as yet seen Dr Lawton that morning. He was decidedly conspicuous by his absence, and in the end she asked Julie Acland where he was.

'He's off duty today,' replied Julie. 'It's different without him, isn't it?'

'Yes,' agreed Pippa as she felt a stab of disappointment. 'Yes, it is.' She wasn't sure that their reasons for thinking this were the same, but she decided not to pursue the matter further.

Julie, however, paused reflectively and looked up from the anti-tetanus ampoules she was checking. 'I don't know what we'd do if he left.'

Pippa looked up sharply. 'Is that likely?' she asked, and found herself holding her breath as she waited for Julie's reply.

The older girl wrinkled her nose. 'I wouldn't have thought so, but old Fortescue, the senior reg, is moving on, so I would imagine Dr Lawton would apply for that post. It's the next logical step for him, but,' she shrugged, 'you never can tell, he's been here for a fair time now and he may decide to apply to another hospital.'

Pippa swallowed and tried to get on with her work, but her concentration had slipped and by the end of the day she was angry with herself for knowing that she had actually missed the registrar's presence about the place. It was as she was clearing up one of the treatment-rooms after an RTA that Hannah Scott asked if she was coming to her party that night.

Pippa smiled and nodded. 'Yes, I'm looking forward to it.'

'Do you know the way to the farmhouse?' asked Hannah.

'It's OK,' said Karen, who had come into the room and overheard. 'I'll pick you up, Pippa.'

'That's kind of you, are you sure it's no bother?'

'Not at all, I have to pass Maple House anyway,' replied Karen.

When Pippa got home there was still no sign of Richard. His flat was silent, and while she got ready for the party Pippa found herself wondering how he'd spent his day off. He'd said he had an appointment at Freelands that evening, but could he have been there all day? Had Mark been right when he'd said it was probably a woman that Richard visited?

Suddenly Pippa felt depressed, and, pulling open the wardrobe door, she scanned her clothes, wondering what she should wear. Maybe, she thought, it was simply a relative he visited, an elderly aunt or a friend of his family. Yes, that was it, it was probably an old friend of his family whom he'd promised he would keep an eye on.

Dubiously she pulled out a culotte suit that she hadn't yet worn. It had cost her a small fortune, and she'd known at the time that she really shouldn't have bought it. It was a soft brushed jersey material in a rich shade of burnt orange. She held it against herself and studied her image in the full-length mirror inside the wardrobe door. It was a perfect foil for her dark hair, olive complexion and brown eyes.

Maybe Richard would have finished his visit early in the evening. Was the outfit too dressy for a party? Again Pippa critically studied her reflection. Perhaps he would get to the party after all.

Suddenly her depression lifted and optimistically she flung the outfit on to the bed and began to undress.

Karen picked her up just before eight o'clock and they drove the ten miles or so to the Scotts' home. The forecourt of the old farmhouse was packed with cars, and as Karen found a space and parked and the two girls climbed out Pippa looked round. But, although she strained her eyes into the darkest corners of the forecourt, she couldn't see one single motorbike.

'My goodness, she's invited more than the Cas crew,' commented Karen as they approached the front door. 'It looks as if half the hospital are here!'

Hannah herself greeted them at the door, looking quite radiant in a cerise caftan and with her blonde hair flowing loose.

The rich panelling of the brightly lit hallway was warm and inviting after the crisp cold outside, and to add to the atmosphere a large Christmas tree, its sole decoration dozens of tiny gold lights, stood at the foot of the stairs.

'Come in, so pleased you could come,' said Hannah. 'Coats upstairs in the first bedroom, food is in the breakfast-room and the bar, of course, is in the kitchen. Please help yourselves, and have fun!'

In the large bedroom Pippa took off her outdoor clothes, then, taking a brush from her bag, she leaned her head forward and brushed her hair from the roots. Then, standing upright, she tossed her head and her hair cascaded down her back in a wild dark cloud. Suddenly she realised that Karen was staring at her.

'What is it?' she asked. 'Is there anything wrong?'

'No. . .no, not at all.' Karen looked slightly bemused. 'It's just that you look so different. In fact, Pippa, you look quite stunning—that outfit is divine, I'm green with envy. . .and your hair. . . I had no idea you had so much. When it's all tucked up under your cap it looks quite severe. Where do you get that wonderful dark colouring from?'

Pippa laughed and, catching sight of herself in the dressing-table mirror, adjusted the loose jacket-style top of her outfit. 'My colouring comes from my grandmother,' she said, then, by way of explanation, she added, 'she was Italian.'

'Ah, that explains it,' said Karen as she renewed her lipstick. 'Shall we go down now?'

Loud music greeted them from the lounge and

dining-room which had been opened up to form one large room, and through the open doors they could see that the party was well under way.

After helping themselves to glasses of spiced punch from the kitchen the two girls made their way to the lounge, where both were soon asked to dance.

For the next couple of hours Pippa hardly left the floor, for no sooner had she finished dancing with one houseman or doctor then she was claimed by another. In the end she wondered just who was on duty at Whitford General that evening, for everyone seemed to be at Hannah Scott's party.

All except one, that was, and as the time crept towards eleven o'clock Pippa was finally forced to accept that he wasn't coming. With a pang she wondered where he was and with whom, and quite against her will she found herself battling with images of him in bed with a glamorous blonde—who she was, she had no idea, but she knew the image would return to haunt her again and again.

So lost was she in her thoughts that she jumped violently, spilling her drink, as someone crept up on her from behind and covered her eyes.

'Guess who?' As he released her she spun round and found Tim laughing down at her.

'Tim! Who invited you? I didn't think there'd be any other students here.' Suddenly she was pleased to see him.

'Oh, I wangled it,' he said evasively. 'Come and have a dance.'

The music was quieter now, vintage Chicago,

and someone had dimmed the lights. For a time Pippa was content to lean against Tim, her head on his shoulder as they moved slowly to the music, then dreamily she became aware that he was murmuring softly against her ear.

'You know, Pippa, that idea I had about us moving in together. . . I don't think it was so bad after all. How about it?'

'No chance,' she murmured back.

'But. . .'

'Forget it.'

'OK.' He pulled her close again and they danced together, closely entwined, for a long time.

It was Tim who finally spoke. 'Is that Karen over there? I think she's looking for you,' he said.

Pippa lifted her head and through the dim light beyond the mass of gently moving couples she saw Karen silhouetted in the open doorway. She was signalling to Pippa.

With a little sigh Pippa pulled away from Tim and they moved slowly towards the door.

'Sorry to be a pain,' said Karen, 'but I really think I should be going.'

'All right,' replied Pippa. 'I'll get my coat.' As she moved forward, a figure suddenly stepped out of the shadows and before she knew what was happening she felt herself being guided back into the darkness of the room.

'It's all right,' a familiar voice explained to Karen and a bemused Tim. 'I shall be taking Philippa home.'

Pippa's heart was thudding wildly as she turned and he pulled her into his arms, then as she caught that deep musky aroma again she sighed, and to the husky sound of Phil Collins she melted against him.

They were silent for a long time, then softly she said, 'I didn't think you were coming.'

'I've been here for some time.'

'You have?' Tilting her head back, she looked up at him, her eyes widening in surprise.

'Yes, I've been watching you. . .'

'And?' she prompted, when the pause seemed to go on forever.

'I couldn't take my eyes off you, you look so beautiful tonight.'

She felt a sharp thrill pierce her body at his words.

'The trouble was everyone else seemed to be of the same opinion,' he went on, then he added drily, 'especially your boyfriend.'

'My boyfriend?' She looked up into his face again, her dark eyes glowing in the half light.

'Well, that's what he is, isn't he?'

His grip had tightened on her and he held her close, pressed against his hard lean body.

'He's a friend, certainly,' she replied teasingly, 'but I certainly wouldn't call him my boyfriend.'

'And yet there was talk of him moving in with you?'

'No,' she said softly, 'there was never any chance of that. What you heard was Tim's idea of a "wishful thinking" type joke.'

He didn't answer, but she sensed he was pleased by her reply, because he moved his hands from her waist, running them over her hips, then

gripping her thighs. She stiffened at the possess-
iveness of his movements and in an almost involuntary gesture she slid her arms around his neck,
linking her fingers just at the point where his dark
hair touched his collar.

He lowered his head slightly and his cheek
rubbed against hers. It felt rough, the stubble
beginning to form, and a tremor of delight rippled
down her spine. She could hardly believe what
was happening. She'd spent the day wondering
about him, where he was and what he was doing,
while at the same time she hadn't wanted to admit,
even to herself, that he as much as occupied a
fraction of her thoughts. Now suddenly, unbeliev-
ably, she was in his arms, and in spite of all the
aggravation there had been between them it felt
right. She felt it was where she belonged and she
wanted it to go on forever; the sensuous beat of
the music, the dim, faintly smoky atmosphere, the
musky aroma she had come to associate with him
and the feel of his hard body.

In the end it was he who broke the spell, and
holding her away from him, he said, 'You love
parties, don't you?'

'Oh, yes, I do,' she smiled, and in a gesture of
pure abandon she tossed her head back in delight,
then, when he didn't comment, with a wicked
flash from her dark eyes she said, 'I gather you
don't.'

'Don't what?'

'Like parties.'

'No, I don't,' he admitted. He was casually
dressed in denims and a polo-necked shirt, and

once again Pippa wondered where he had been earlier.

'So why did you come?' she whispered daringly.

He stared down at her, his features only half visible in the dim light. 'I would have thought that was pretty obvious,' he murmured, and roughly pulled her closer again.

The magic of the moment was finally destroyed as the tempo of the music changed from its slow smoochy rhythm to a fast disco beat and the room was suddenly invaded by a crush of people.

Richard pulled a face. 'Shall we go?'

Pippa nodded, and with his arm still around her they left the room. In the hall he released her and in the sudden brightness they stared at each other in a kind of wonder.

'I'll get my coat,' she whispered at last, and, turning away from him, she climbed the stairs, only too aware that he stood below watching her until she reached the landing.

In the bedroom she rifled through the coats until she found her own, then, catching sight of her reflection in the mirror, she paused. Her cheeks were flushed, her dark eyes shone with an excitement that wasn't only to do with the prospect of another ride on the motorbike, and her lips were parted in a breathless smile. With a little sigh of pure pleasure she pulled on her coat and hurried down to the hall again to join Richard for the ride back to Maple House.

CHAPTER NINE

To PIPPA it was a magical night, for although it seemed highly unlikely that she would see the much-longed-for snow the air was crisp with a white frost. They had said goodbye to Hannah and slipped away unnoticed from the party, which was threatening to go on well into the early hours. At any other time Pippa would have wanted to stay to the end for the bacon sandwiches served just before dawn, but tonight was different and nothing on earth could have stopped her going with Richard.

Whether or not Tim noticed, or for that matter any of the others from the casualty staff, she didn't know, neither did she care. All that mattered was the man in front of her, as she slipped her arms around his waist and rested her face against the smooth leather of his jacket.

He drove slowly through the country lanes, for in places the surfaces were icy, between blackthorn hedges that glittered in the bike's headlight, while ahead the road resembled a shining ribbon, the granite chippings in the tarmac glistening in the moonlight.

Not a word had passed between them as Richard handed her the spare helmet and she had wrapped herself up against the cold. But somehow there had been no need for words, and for the ten-mile ride home Pippa was content to hold him while the powerful engine purred beneath them.

Then too soon they were home, and Richard rode the bike straight to the garage at the back of the house. As they walked to the house together Pippa found her whole body clenched with tension as she wondered what would happen next.

Richard had now made it quite plain that he found her attractive, and he now also knew that Tim wasn't her boyfriend. She had no idea what his next move would be, or whether or not he would even make a move. Neither did she know how she would react to any such move. Although Pippa had had plenty of boyfriends in the past, that was what they had been—boys, while Richard Lawton was a man, a much older man and, to complicate matters further, her CO into the bargain.

The house was in darkness and very quiet, as he followed her through the hall and up the stairs. Again neither of them spoke, then as they reached the landing Richard paused, and Pippa held her breath.

'I believe it's my turn to make coffee,' he said quietly, and as he fitted his key into the lock she felt a quiver of excitement run the length of her spine.

She hadn't seen the inside of his flat before, and she looked round with interest as he lit the lamps and put a tape into the deck, then, stepping towards her, he said, 'Shall I take your coat?'

Awkwardly she struggled out of her coat and he took it, then disappeared into another room. His flat seemed larger than hers, and she guessed it

was more than a bedsit and that the room beyond
was his bedroom. She still felt very tense, and in
an effort to relax she sat down on the sofa and
looked round at his possessions. She knew very
little about him and was curious to see if his flat
gave any clues to his personality. The furniture
was black and modern, geometric in design with
plenty of glass and tubular steel, and Pippa
guessed it was his own and not hospital issue. The
bookshelves were crammed with books which at a
glance appeared to be mainly medical, the heavy
oak desk supported a word processor, and there
were very few pictures or ornaments. The only
true reflection on Richard's preferences seemed to
come from the tape that was playing softly, and
vaguely Pippa recognised a Chopin nocturne—a
favourite of her father's.

A little later he returned with two mugs of
coffee. He had taken off his leather jacket, but to
her disappointment instead of sitting beside her
on the sofa he sat opposite in an armchair.

In the silence that followed she desperately
sought for something to say. 'Have you had your
motorbike for very long?' she asked at last. She
didn't really want to know, but she felt she had to
break the embarrassing silence.

He shook his head. 'No, not this particular one.'

'You mean there've been others?'

He smiled, the skin crinkling at the corners of
his eyes, and she felt her throat constrict as she
watched him. 'Oh, yes, many others,' he replied,
taking a mouthful of his coffee, then setting the
mug down on the glass-topped coffee-table.

He glanced across at her, and, seeing her look

of interest, he went on, 'My brother and I were motorbike fanatics—you know the sort of thing, bits of machines all over the place, even in the house.'

'Your poor mother!' Pippa leaned forward, sipping her coffee. She suddenly felt more relaxed and she felt that he too seemed less tense.

'I don't know how she put up with us,' he grinned, and paused as if reflecting on his boyhood days, then the smile left his face. 'After Danny was killed motorbikes were banned, not that I particularly wanted to ride any more.'

'How old were you when your brother died?'

'Eighteen. He was only sixteen. Afterwards I threw myself into my studies. There was only Mum and me then—my father had died when Danny and I were kids. My mother took two jobs to get me through medical school.'

'She must be very proud of you now.' Pippa finished her coffee and replaced her mug on the table.

'Yes, I suppose she is, but I haven't finished yet. . .' He lapsed into silence, but for a second Pippa caught a fleeting glimpse of raw determination on his features and she knew all the rumours she had heard about him were true; about his being a workaholic, a perfectionist, and of how he wouldn't be satisfied until he reached the very peak of his career.

They lapsed into silence again, and when Pippa glanced up she realised that while she had been reflecting about him he had been watching her. Their eyes met and their gaze held, but Pippa found his expression impossible to read, then with a sound that was a cross between a groan and a sigh he stood up.

'I suppose we'd better call it a day,' he muttered. 'It could be busy tomorrow, being Christmas Eve.'

With a deep pang of disappointment she watched him as he went to get her coat. When he came back he held the coat open for her and she turned away so that he could help her put it on. As he slid it over her shoulders her cloud of dark hair became trapped, and she stiffened as she felt him slip his hands inside the coat, attempting to free her hair, but when at last she shook it free, he didn't move away, neither did he take his hands from her shoulders.

She stood motionless, hardly daring to breathe, as his grip tightened, then with a muffled sound he turned her to face him. She had time only to look up into his face; to get a brief glimpse of the look of hunger in his grey eyes before his hands moved from her shoulders to either side of her head, becoming entwined in her hair, holding her face upturned to his, before his mouth came down on hers.

It was a kiss like no other she had ever known; a kiss that started softly, gently, questioningly, the merest touch of his lips against hers, then increased in pressure and exploration to a kiss so full of fire and passion that it left her senses reeling.

Then as the demands of his lips increased, evoking desires deep within her whose existence she had never even suspected, she found herself responding with an intensity that shocked and amazed her.

She would never have believed possible the fervency of desire that uncoiled inside her. It was like something that had lain dormant all her life simply waiting for that exquisite moment of awakening.

His kiss went on seemingly forever, there was no measure of time or place, only the blissful ecstasy of the moment, the sweetness of his mouth, the grip of his arms and the pressure of his taut hard body against hers.

Then it was over, her fantasy flown, and he almost thrust her from him in an agony of despair.

Breathless and panting, they faced each other, at first shocked at the unexpected intensity of their passion, then warily, like two animals, adversaries in the game of love, then with an anguished sound, Richard said, 'Please go, Philippa. . .'

Her reply equalled his for passion. 'But why. . .?'

'Because I could never be responsible for my actions if you were to stay.'

'Then why. . .?'

'Just go.'

Miserably, in an agony of despair, she left him, but later, as she lay wakeful in her bed, she slowly began to recover, to revel in the fact that there had been no denying that, for that brief moment at least, he had wanted her as much as she had wanted him.

And it was then that she knew what she had been unable to admit even to herself; she was in love with Richard Lawton.

* * *

Pippa was still in a daze the next morning when she arrived at Casualty but, after the previous night's party, so was everyone else, so her vagueness almost went unnoticed. The only one who showed any interest was Karen.

Pippa was restocking the dressings and other supplies in the treatment-rooms, and her nerves were stretched to breaking point because she hadn't as much as caught a glimpse of Richard that morning. She glanced up sharply as Karen came into the room carrying a pile of blankets, then as she saw her expression she hurriedly looked away.

Karen, however, was not to be put off. 'What time did you get home last night?' she asked as she began sorting the blankets.

'I'm not really sure,' Pippa mumbled. 'I think it was around midnight.'

'You went home on the motorbike?'

'Yes,' she replied briefly, then thought that really she should say something more, for, after all, Karen had been good enough to take her to the party in the first place. 'I hope you didn't mind my not coming with you, Karen,' she said.

The older girl shrugged. 'Not at all. I suppose it made sense really, with Dr Lawton and you living in the same house.' She paused and Pippa wished she would change the subject, but instead she went on, 'I was surprised to see him at the party in the first place, I can't ever remember seeing him at a staff party before. I expect it was because it was Hannah's,' she mused.

Fortunately, at that moment Derek Henderson stuck his head round the door and called Karen to a cubicle where a woman was having an epileptic fit. Pippa mercifully was left alone.

For the rest of the morning she assisted with minor dressings, of which there were plenty in spite of it being Christmas Eve. There also seemed to be much activity in A and E, and Derek explained that that was because of the increased volume of traffic resulting in several RTAs, with so many people trying to get to their homes for Christmas.

By mid-morning she still hadn't seen Richard, and she felt quite sick with apprehension. She imagined he must be in A and E but was so busy that she just hadn't seen him, then about eleven o'clock Sister Gould asked her to take some folders to Derek Henderson. With her heart thumping Pippa stopped before the double doors, then, taking a deep breath, she pushed them open and walked in.

The staff were grouped around a patient on one of the couches. They looked up as Pippa came in, and to her amazement she saw that the doctor was Dr Patel, Dr Lawton's locum. She handed over the folders to Derek, then went back to Reception with her mind reeling. Where was Richard? Was he ill? He'd quite definitely said he would be on duty that morning.

By the time she rejoined Karen in the dressing cubicles she had to know. As casually as she could she said, 'Dr Patel's over on A and E. They seem pretty busy; isn't Dr Lawton on duty?'

Karen threw her a sharp glance and she felt the colour stain her cheeks. 'He's in a meeting with senior management.'

'Oh. . .?'

Karen hesitated, as if wondering how much she
should say, then she shrugged. 'You'll know soon
enough anyway, so I may as well tell you.'

Pippa felt as if her nerves were stretched to
breaking point as she waited to hear what Karen
was going to say.

'Mr Fortescue, the senior registrar, has just been
offered a consultancy, so his post here will be
vacant. No doubt they're discussing the position
with Dr Lawton.'

'Isn't it a foregone conclusion that he'll get it?'
asked Pippa.

'Probably, but it isn't as straightforward as that.
Rumour has it,' again Karen hesitated and glanced
shrewdly at Pippa, 'that an even better post has
become vacant in Edinburgh. Dr Lawton may well
consider that.'

'Edinburgh?' There was no disguising the
dismay on Pippa's face as she stared at Karen.

Karen was silent for a moment, then, stretching
out her hand, she flicked the curtains of the empty
cubicle around them. 'Pippa,' her voice was low
with a trace of urgency, 'you're not getting
involved with Dr Lawton, are you?'

Pippa stared at her, then gave a brittle laugh.
'Whatever gave you that idea? He doesn't even
like me—haven't you noticed how he's always on
at me?'

'That may be, but it's not him I'm talking about,
it's you, and I saw your face when he appeared
last night. But if you've got any ideas, Pippa,
forget them,' said Karen brutally. 'You wouldn't
be the first, believe me. There've been plenty

who've thought they could break through that ice-cold exterior. But none have ever got anywhere, and most have ended up very hurt. He's either committed elsewhere, or he just doesn't want to get involved. So just take a tip from me, Pippa, and leave well alone where Richard Lawton's concerned.' With that Karen flung back the curtains and strode off down the corridor, leaving Pippa wondering if she had been one of those who had tried to break through the ice-cold exterior and been rebuffed.

Pippa shivered slightly; there might well be an ice-cold exterior to Richard Lawton, but she had experienced the fire that lay beneath.

Throughout the afternoon she worried about what Karen had said, not about the fact that the older girl had warned her not to become involved—it was too late for that, she was already more involved than she had ever been in her life—but that he might be considering a move to Edinburgh. She knew how ambitious he was and that if he was offered something that would further his career even more he wouldn't hesitate in taking it. And then again, there had been that elusive reference to the possibility of another woman in his life, and at that prospect she was filled with an even greater agony.

Casualty became a little quieter after lunch and the Christmas parties that had been going on in every office, in every hospital department, began to get into full swing.

At three o'clock Sister Gould told Pippa that as she was on duty the following day she could go home. When Pippa reached the changing-room she heard Derek Henderson telling another charge nurse that Dr Patel would be taking Dr Lawton's place for the rest of the day as Dr Lawton also was on duty on Christmas Day.

As Pippa hurried from the unit she resigned herself to the fact that she wouldn't be seeing Richard that day unless he was around at home that evening. She knew, however, that Sue Robinson was organising a Christmas drink in the reception-room at Maple House, and that was something that Richard would probably avoid.

As she reached her car she smiled grimly as it occurred to her that already she seemed to be a pretty good judge of Richard's likes and dislikes.

Unlocking her car, she decided that as she was so early she would go into town and do some last-minute shopping, but as she was fastening her seatbelt she heard a shout, and glancing up, saw Claire running towards her across the car park.

She wound down her window. 'Claire, I thought you'd gone,' she said anxiously, adding, 'You are still going home, aren't you?'

'Yes, I'm just leaving now. That ratbag of a sister wouldn't let me go before—she kept reminding me that there were some who had to work over Christmas and that I was lucky to be going home. Lucky—huh! If only she knew!'

'Did you see our tutor?'

Claire nodded. 'Yes, she said more or less the same as you and that I had to talk it through with my father but that she would offer any help or advice that she could.'

Pippa nodded. 'Good, I thought that's what

she'd say; she wouldn't want to lose you, Claire.
Now, when do you get back?'

'The twenty-seventh.' Claire paused, and, leaning forward, stared at Pippa critically. 'That's
enough about me—what about you?'

'What about me?'

'You look shattered.'

Pippa shrugged. 'Oh, I'm all right. Late night,
that's all.'

'Oh, that's right, it was Dr Scott's party, wasn't
it? It's been the talk of the hospital today. Did you
enjoy it?'

'Oh, yes,' replied Pippa casually.

Claire narrowed her eyes. 'So what's wrong,
then? Come on, Pippa, I know you too well, and
there's something wrong.'

'It's nothing, honestly,' Pippa lied. There was
no way she was going to add to her friend's
problems by burdening her with her own.

Claire glanced at her watch. 'Look, I have to fly
now if I'm going to get to Shrewsbury, but I want
to know what this is all about the moment I get
back, OK?'

Pippa smiled and nodded. 'OK—and, Claire, try
and enjoy Christmas.'

She watched as her friend pulled a face and
hurried away. She might have known that Claire
would have noticed a change in her, for hadn't
she, Pippa, detected when something had been
wrong in her friend's life? As Claire had said, they
had been close for a long time and had come to
know each other's moods very well.

The weather that day had turned much milder,
and there was a decided dampness in the air as

Pippa parked her car in the multi-storey in town and made her way down to the brightly lit shopping area.

The town was packed with people frantically stocking up with last-minute items of festive food and drink, and as Pippa watched the hustle and bustle she felt a moment's loneliness. This would be like no other Christmas she had ever known, and suddenly she longed for her family, so far away on the other side of the world. As if to add to her sudden wave of nostalgia, a Salvation Army band grouped around the entrance to Woolworths suddenly struck up with an old familiar Christmas carol, and Pippa was forced to swallow a lump in her throat.

She finished her shopping and was just waiting to cross the busy main road to go back to the car park when a large group of motorcyclists caught her eye. They were parked in a long line in a bay in front of the public library, and for a moment Pippa found herself enviously watching them. She had enjoyed her motorbike rides—much to her surprise, because it had never been something she had been particularly keen to do in the past. But there had been a thrill and exhilaration about it that had amazed and delighted her.

There were several girls in the group, their gear of black leather jackets and blue jeans identical to the boys'. One girl in particular stood out. She was leaning against a red motorbike and her long blonde hair cascaded down her back. She was surrounded by a group of boys, but she was laughing up at one particular person who was partly hidden by one of the stone pillars in front of the library. As the group parted the blonde girl's companion stepped into Pippa's line of vision, and with a sickening jolt Pippa realised it was Richard.

CHAPTER TEN

FOR a moment Pippa remained rooted to the spot, her brain almost incapable of taking in the scene, then, biting her lip, she put her head down in the hope that Richard wouldn't see her and hurriedly crossed the road.

He didn't come to Sue's party that evening, and by the time Pippa went to bed she had convinced herself he was still with the blonde girl. Although she had had her suspicions that he might be involved with a woman she had been amazed to see how young the girl was, probably still in her teens and not at all the type of woman Pippa would have expected Richard to choose. . .but then, she thought, as she tossed and turned, trying to get to sleep but listening for the sound of his return, she herself was only twenty. . .

As her thoughts revolved she found herself trying to make up her mind just what kind of woman she would have expected him to choose. Someone sophisticated, maybe? But that didn't quite fit. Someone with interests similar to his own? Now that did fit; the girl he'd been with looked very much into the motorbike scene. Pippa groaned and buried her face in the pillow. And then again, although she knew Richard was a motorbike fanatic, she hadn't visualised him as being part of a gang. . .that simply didn't fit at all, because everyone said what a loner he was.

But the one question that returned again and again in her mind, preventing her sleeping until well into the early hours, was why had he acted in the way he had with her, Pippa? If he really was involved elsewhere why had he come to Hannah's party? Why had he insisted on taking her home, and, most important of all, why had he kissed her in the way he had?

Eventually she must have slept, because when she awoke it was a grey Christmas dawn and she hadn't heard Richard come home after all. Wearily she got out of bed, made some tea, then climbed back into bed and eyed the little pile of presents she'd received from her family and friends.

Once again she was swamped by a feeling of loneliness and homesickness; this was like no other Christmas she'd ever known, and even the thought of the belated celebration promised for her parents' return did little to raise her spirits.

Blinking back the sudden tears that threatened, she reached out for the first brightly wrapped parcel.

By the time she had showered, dressed and eaten her breakfast she was feeling a little better, but she was glad to get out of the house and drive to work.

There were several agency and relief staff on duty in Casualty, but Pippa was pleased to find that Sister Gould was there. 'Do you think we're likely to be busy?' she asked the older woman after they had exchanged Christmas greetings.

'It's hard to tell—it's usually one drunk after another, victims of domestic violence, and the overdoses, of course.'

Pippa raised her eyebrows questioningly.

'We have more ODs at Christmas than at any other time of the year. It's a terrible time for depressives, seeing everyone else supposedly enjoying themselves. For some it just proves to be too much—speaking of which, what are you doing when you get off duty?'

'Oh, I shall go to the social club, most likely,' replied Pippa, then trailed off as Sister Gould glanced over her shoulder. 'Ah, here's Dr Lawton. Merry Christmas, Richard,' she said.

Pippa turned sharply, and at the sight of his smile her heart stood still. She hadn't heard him come in, and he was standing quite close behind her.

'Good morning, Rose,' he said. 'Merry Christmas, and to you, Philippa.' He'd dropped the formalities that morning, and with a beam Sister Gould bustled off to Reception, leaving him and Pippa alone in the office.

'I overheard what you said just now, Philippa, about going to the social club,' he said.

She shrugged. 'I might as well. Claire's gone home for Christmas.'

He hesitated briefly. 'I was wondering if you'd like to have dinner with me. I'm on my own as well, and, quite frankly, I don't think anyone should be on their own on Christmas night.'

Suddenly she felt as if her senses were singing. 'Thank you Richard, I'd love to,' she replied, trying hard to keep her voice under control.

She didn't know how she got through the rest of the day, especially as it proved to be emotionally demanding. Sister Gould, speaking from years of experience, had been quite correct when she had predicted what they could expect. By midday they had dealt with more than their fair share of drunks, two RTAs, both involving children on new bicycles, an acute appendicitis and three overdoses.

As she assisted with the stomach wash-out of a young man in his thirties she found, deep within herself, a glimmer of understanding for what he had attempted. Had she too not felt alone and depressed that morning? But she had family and friends, and she could only imagine what it must be like to be without either.

Richard was kinder to her that day than he had ever been, although once they had left the office and entered A and E he had reverted to calling her Nurse Ward again.

Then at last her duty was over, and as she was buttoning her coat Richard put his head round the door. 'Have you got your car?' he asked, and, when she nodded, he added, 'Can you be ready about seven?'

'Yes—oh, yes!' she answered, then as he disappeared back into the office she felt her stomach churn with excitement.

Maple House was quiet and deserted when she arrived home, for most of the residents had returned to their families for Christmas. Pippa had been quite resigned to staying at the hospital and going to the social club with the rest of the duty staff if Richard hadn't asked her out, but, as it was, she couldn't wait to find something suitable to wear and get herself ready.

Her burnt orange suit was the nicest thing she

had, but he had already seen her in that, so anxiously she pulled out her other clothes and tried several matchings before she decided on an emerald-green skirt with a black printed pattern, a silky black shirt and a large coloured scarf in bright jewel colours that she fastened on one shoulder with a leopard-shaped brooch.

Her hair she caught up high on either side of her head with two gold combs, and for the final effect she added a pair of gold hoop earrings. It was while she was spraying herself with her favourite perfume that it suddenly occurred to her that she might have difficulty on the motorbike with her skirt, which was very full and almost ankle-length. But she needn't have worried, because when she opened the door to Richard, he suggested that as it was such a mild night they might walk to the restaurant he had chosen for their meal.

They strolled together through the almost deserted streets past rows of houses, some in darkness and others with lighted trees in their windows. The sound of Pippa's heels echoed in the still night air, and she wished Richard would take her hand or even hold her arm, but he did neither. He looked casual and very handsome in dark cord trousers and a tan-coloured suede jacket. He wasn't wearing his glasses, and Pippa came to the conclusion that he only seemed to wear them for his work or for reading.

Once or twice she managed to steal a glance at him as they walked, and she found it difficult to believe that he had actually asked her out. Fleetingly she wondered about the blonde girl, then she decided she wouldn't let thoughts of her spoil her own evening. She did her best to banish the image she had of the girl, with her head thrown back and her fair hair tumbling over her black leather jacket as she'd laughed up into Richard's face.

The restaurant was only a few streets away from Maple House, and Pippa was pleased to see it was Italian. They were greeted by the proprietor, Salvatore, who seemed to know Richard rather well. He showed them to a candlelit table in a secluded alcove and took their order for drinks.

'Do you approve of my choice?' asked Richard, as Salvatore disappeared behind the bar.

'Oh, yes.' Pippa looked round the restaurant, at the tasteful wall murals depicting scenes of old Tuscany, the dark-haired waiters who seemed to glide around the other diners and the soft intimate glow from the candlelight. 'In fact you couldn't have chosen anywhere nicer—I adore Italian food.'

After they had ordered their pasta dishes they talked shop, and Richard asked her if there was any particular area in which she hoped to specialise.

'I'm not sure yet,' replied Pippa thoughtfully. 'I don't think I'll attempt to decide until I've finished my training.'

'That's wise,' he replied. 'You need to gain as much experience as you can before you make any lasting decisions.' He paused fractionally, and briefly her eyes met his. 'How are you enjoying Casualty now?'

'Very much,' she replied, then, considering carefully, she added, 'But I do find it emotionally draining.'

'It is,' he agreed.

At that moment their food arrived and they were silent until the waiter had left them alone again, then Pippa said, 'Sometimes I wonder if I have what it takes to be a good casualty nurse.' She gave a short laugh. 'Or, come to that, any sort of nurse!'

She was staring at the red tablecloth as she spoke, and when he didn't answer she glanced up at him from beneath her dark lashes. At the look in his eyes her heart seemed to skip a beat.

'You care,' he said briefly, 'and I think that's the single most important quality for being a good nurse.'

She could hardly believe what she was hearing, and she felt her face glow at his praise.

'Having said that,' he mused, staring at her across the flame of the candle, 'I think you still need to learn discipline.'

She pulled a face, then suddenly he laughed and said, 'That's quite enough shop talk, especially for Christmas night.' He glanced round as he spoke. 'Not that it's very traditional in here.' He jerked his head slightly towards the sound of the background music, an Italian tenor singing a passionate aria.

'I don't mind; I haven't felt very traditional this Christmas,' Pippa told him. 'Besides, I like that music, it's so romantic.'

'Romantic? Yes, I suppose it is. There's so little time for romance in my life that I guess I just don't recognise it any more.'

He spoke in a light-hearted tone which must have given her courage, for she found herself saying, 'Not even with the glamorous blonde I saw you with?'

He frowned, and in the silence which followed Pippa wished she could have bitten out her tongue, then carefully he set down his fork and looked quizzically at her over the candle flame. There was a sudden draught as someone opened a door somewhere and the flame danced frantically, throwing shadows that gave his dark features a sardonic look.

'I beg your pardon?' he said quietly.

Pippa swallowed. 'The blonde girl. . .yesterday in town. I saw you outside the library. . .' She trailed off miserably, then to her relief he suddenly laughed.

'Oh, you mean Leyla?'

'Leyla?' she echoed, and her voice came out barely more than a whisper. She desperately wished she'd kept her mouth shut, for suddenly she had the feeling he was going to tell her something she didn't want to hear.

'Yes, that was Leyla O'Rourke—she lives up on the Freelands estate.'

Freelands—there it was again, the place she had heard the gossip about concerning Richard. Suddenly she realised he was staring at her, and she threw him a half-fearful glance.

'You didn't think. . .?' he began, then stopped, but continued to stare at her. Then he shook his head as if suddenly amused by something. He didn't, however, comment any further, and Pippa was left still wondering as they continued with their meal.

There was a light mist forming haloes round the street lamps as they left Salvatore's, and Richard paused, one foot on the kerb, and glanced at his watch. 'You were asking earlier about Leyla,' he said quietly.

Pippa felt her mouth go suddenly dry and she wondered what he was about to tell her. Dumbly she nodded.

'I'd like to take you over to Freelands if you have the time.' When she nodded again in reply he went on, 'We'll go back to Maple House and get the bike.'

She'd been right about one thing—her long skirt was a problem when she tried to mount the motorbike, but at last she managed to tuck it beneath her, then they were roaring off through the deserted streets and she knew with a growing sense of dread that she was about to find out whatever or whoever it was that took up so much of Richard's time on the Freelands estate.

Many new housing projects were under way on the vast estate, but as they drove slowly through the empty streets Pippa could see in the light from the overhead street lamps that many properties had become run-down and were boarded up and derelict. Some buildings had been badly vandalised, their windows broken, slates ripped from the roofs and graffiti daubed on the walls.

Occasionally a lighted Christmas tree glowed cheerfully from a darkened window, a sudden reminder to Pippa of what day it was and of how this was surely the strangest Christmas she had ever spent. They hardly encountered a soul on their drive through the dark streets; once a dog came out of an alley barking furiously at them and chasing the bike down the street, and at one corner Richard had to swerve to avoid a drunk who lurched dangerously in the gutter. As they penetrated further and further into the maze of streets Pippa felt her apprehension growing. Why was Richard bringing her here? He'd mentioned Leyla almost as if he was taking her to meet the blonde girl, but who was she? If she was indeed his girlfriend, as Pippa feared and as the hospital gossip had implied, then she knew she didn't want to meet her. But she was still puzzled by the whole thing; something didn't quite ring true, but she wasn't sure what it was. She knew Richard wasn't a snob, but somehow he just didn't seem to fit in with these surroundings.

She shivered slightly as the blackened buildings seemed to crowd in on her, then suddenly they had rounded a corner and Richard had brought the bike to a halt before a large red-brick building that looked like a church. Light spilled out on to the pavement through the double doors and from the many stained glass windows, while a deep throbbing sound filled the air and made the ground vibrate beneath them.

Richard dismounted, pulled off his crash helmet, then turned and helped her to dismount. As she lifted her own helmet Pippa realised that the throbbing sound was in fact music, but music played so loud that the whole building seemed to be shaking.

Richard pulled a face and held out his hand to her. 'Can you bear to come inside?'

Mystified, she followed him, then she saw the rows of motorbikes lined up at the side of the building, just like the ones she'd seen the day before outside the library in town.

The hall, which was indeed a converted church, was packed with leather-jacketed teenagers. Some were sitting at tables littered with Coke cans, while others lounged against the walls, smoking and chatting. The heavy metal music they had heard from outside blared forth from an old-fashioned, sixties-style jukebox, and two girls in skin-tight jeans and leather jackets were dancing in the centre of the floor. One of them had short, jet-black spiky hair, and when she turned Pippa could see a tiger's head emblem on the back of her jacket, but it was her companion who finally caught her attention. She too wore tight jeans and the customary black leather, but her hair was fair and it cascaded down her back in a wild tangled mass. As she turned a smile crossed her slightly sulky features as she caught sight of Richard, and with a pang Pippa saw it was Leyla and that she was indeed very young.

More confused than ever now, Pippa half turned to Richard, hoping for some explanation as to why he had brought her to this place and what his involvement was with these young people, but before either of them had a chance to utter a word a shout went up from the back of the hall.

'Hey, it's the doc! Hi there, Doc, we didn't expect you tonight.' A large man with a shock of ginger hair and a bushy beard was making his way towards them across the hall. He too was dressed in the leathers that seemed to be the uniform of these people and his jeans were smeared with engine grease and oil, but he appeared older than the others, probably in his late thirties, Pippa thought.

'Hello there, Cameron—Merry Christmas to you. I've brought a friend to meet you. This is Philippa.'

Pippa was vaguely aware that the music had stopped and in the silence she heard a smothered giggle from one of the girls. She felt the colour flood her cheeks, then her hand was grasped in a huge paw-like grip and Cameron was beaming down at her. She noticed he had a couple of teeth missing, but his smile was friendly.

'Welcome to the Freewheelers. . .any friend of Doc's. . .' He trailed off as someone else suddenly shouted from across the hall.

'Doc, will you have a quick look at me bike? It's playin' up again.' A tall thin-faced boy had left the table where he had been sitting with his mates and had come across to them.

'Yes, OK, Scott,' replied Richard amiably. 'We'll take a look now, shall we?' He gave Pippa an apologetic smile. 'Won't be a minute,' he said. 'Cameron will look after you.'

Pippa watched in dismay as he disappeared out of the main doors.

'Won't be a minute,' mimicked Cameron. 'Heard that one before. . .more like an hour, I should think!'

'An hour?' Pippa stared at him.

'Well, you know the doc, once he gets stuck into a bike he loses all track of time.'

'Does he?' said Pippa faintly.

'That he does. . .there ain't nothin' the Doc don't know about bikes. Now how about a drink?'

'A drink? Oh, yes, thank you,' said Pippa, trying to pull herself together as she followed the huge figure of Cameron to a table where he handed her a can of Coke. She stared at it for a moment, horribly conscious that the others all seemed to be watching her, almost as if they were waiting for her to ask for a glass. Taking a deep breath, she pulled the ring on the can, then putting the tin to her lips took a large mouthful. Spluttering a little, she wiped some of the fizzy liquid as it trickled down her chin, then as she grinned at Cameron, someone put another record on the jukebox, conversation resumed and she ceased to be the centre of attention.

'Are you Doc's girlfriend?'

Pippa swung round and found the girl Leyla standing close behind her. She noticed she had beautiful green eyes and she had threaded a piece of tinsel through her hair. There was a suspicious expression on her features as she eyed Pippa up and down.

'Oh, no,' Pippa said quickly. 'We simply work together in Casualty. I'm a nurse.' She was immediately aware of a lessening of tension in the other girl's attitude and wondered anew what the relationship was between Leyla and Richard. 'Do you know him very well?' she asked curiously.

The other girl stared at her as if she was mad.

'Of course we do. He got us this place.' She waved her hand, indicating the hall.

'Did he?' Pippa looked bewildered, then Cameron broke in after taking a swig from his own can of Coke and indicating for her to take a seat opposite him.

'Don't you know about the doc and the kids round here?' he asked, and, when she shook her head, he went on, 'He's done more for the kids in this area than anyone else I know. He comes up here in his time off and gives them lessons on riding their bikes, then if they have any problems with the machines I'm damned if he don't put them right too. He got this place for the kids an' all, and had it turned into a youth centre. He even got me the job of runnin' things. . .but that's another story. The kids idolise him, but there's one thing he won't stand for; he won't have no booze in here, not while they're ridin' their machines. . .that's why you'll only find this stuff on the premises.' Cameron took another long drink from his can of Coke, then noisily wiped his mouth with the back of his hand. By this time Leyla and two of the others had sat down as well and begun asking Pippa questions about her work in Casualty.

'I thought I might like to be a nurse once,' said Leyla.

'How old are you?' asked Pippa curiously.

'Sixteen,' the girl replied, and Pippa smiled to herself. How could she have ever imagined that Richard was involved with this girl? Although, she had to admit, Leyla looked a good three or four years older than her sixteen years.

By the time that Richard returned she was talking on friendly terms to several of the young people, and when he gave her a sheepish grin at having kept her waiting so long she merely smiled back, a sudden lump in her throat as she watched him and recalled the things she had just heard about him.

Much later after they had left the hall, ridden back through the stillness of that strange Christmas night, and Richard had put the bike in the garage and joined her in the lane at the side of Maple House, he said, 'Has that answered your question about Leyla?'

'It has,' she laughed softly. 'I thought you and she. . .'

'I know that's what you thought. . .just as I suspect there's been gossip about me on the unit. I've never told anyone else about it,' Richard said quietly.

'But why?' She glanced up at him. Only his profile was visible in the street light.

He shrugged. 'I don't know. It wasn't something I could explain. I suppose that's why I took you over there, to show you.'

'How did you first become involved?'

He hesitated, then slowly he began to explain. 'You remember I told you about my brother's death? Well, afterwards I didn't ride a motorbike for years. I suppose I tried to shut the whole thing out of my mind. But what I hadn't realised was that I suppose I hadn't come to terms with it. I had this dreadful feeling, you see, that my mother blamed me for Danny's death.'

'Oh, surely not. . .how could she?'

'I don't know, maybe because I was the oldest and Danny followed me and copied everything I did.'

'Even so,' she protested.

'I know, but the feeling wouldn't go away. Oh, Mum never said anything, ever, but. . .anyway, I gave up motorbikes and dedicated myself to reaching the very top of my profession, trying to repay her, I suppose, for all her hard work in putting me through medical school.' He was silent for a moment as if reflecting on his past, then slowly he continued, 'It was when I came to work on Casualty that it was all brought back in the worst possible way.' There was a catch in his voice and he paused, and suddenly Pippa wanted to reach out and touch him, to hold him.

'I saw so many accidents involving young boys on motorbikes, many because of drink but just as many because of ignorance and lack of proper tuition. A young lad could have a machine for his sixteenth birthday and take it on the road that day, and some ended up in the mortuary within a week. I decided I wanted to do something about it. I began to realise that many of the victims came from Freelands where there's a high population of teenagers, but I also knew I wouldn't be welcome if I just poked my nose in as another do-gooder, so I decided the best thing I could do was to join them. That's when I bought my bike and took to the road again. I knew I'd win their respect with a good bike, so I bought the best one I could afford. . .not that I haven't enjoyed myself. It was great to be back in the saddle again.'

'And Cameron? Where did he fit in?' They had

reached the entrance to Maple House now, and Pippa paused with her key in the lock and glanced back at Richard over her shoulder.

'Ah, Cameron was a patient.'

'Another accident?'

'No, although he was a member of a Hell's Angels chapter—no, Cameron was an alcoholic. After he'd dried out, I offered him the job running the centre that I'd set up for the kids, and I'm glad to say that to date he hasn't touched a drop. Whether it'll last, I don't know, but I hope so. They'll need someone, especially if I'm not going to be around.'

Pippa stopped dead, then slowly turned. She could only see his silhouette in the open doorway with the street light behind him.

'Are you going somewhere?' she asked, and her voice came out as barely more than a whisper.

'I've applied for a post in Edinburgh,' he replied quietly. 'I have an interview the day after tomorrow.'

CHAPTER ELEVEN

PIPPA stared at Richard in dismay, and he must have interpreted the look in her dark eyes, for he leaned forward and gently ran the back of his fingers down her cheek.

'But why?' she whispered. 'Why Edinburgh?'

They had reached the small landing between their flats and because of the lack of space were standing close together.

He shrugged slightly. 'Because it's too good a post to turn down.'

Pippa blinked and tried to swallow the lump that had risen in her throat.

'And because I think it would be for the best. This can never be, Philippa.' His voice was husky now and once more he stroked her cheek. For one wild moment she thought he was going to kiss her as he had before, and briefly she closed her eyes in a torment of anticipation, but instead he dropped his hand to his side and took a step backwards, then he turned and with a muttered goodnight disappeared into his flat.

Pippa could hardly believe it as his door shut firmly behind him. She had been going to invite him in for coffee, but he hadn't given her the opportunity, and she stared in dismay at the closed door. This certainly wasn't how she had visualised the evening ending.

Consumed by disappointment, she went slowly

into her own flat, closed the door and leaned against it for a moment as she tried to come to terms with what had happened.

When Richard had asked her out she had been ecstatic, for she had hoped he wanted more to come of their relationship. Her main fear had been that he was committed elsewhere, but then when she had realised there was no other involvement she had really begun to hope he was as attracted to her as she was to him.

When he had kissed her after Hannah's party she had been convinced that the intense feeling that had passed between them had been mutual. The fact that he had chosen to confide in her and had taken her to see his work at Freelands had further led her to believe that the relationship between them was becoming special. Then had come his bombshell about the job in Edinburgh. He had even hinted that it was because of their relationship that he was going away, but he had also implied that the post was too good to turn down. Pippa blinked back hot angry tears; everything she had heard about him was true; he was indeed a workaholic, and nothing would be allowed to come between him and the furthering of his beloved career. Somehow he had implied that there could never be anything between them. Was this simply because she was a student? Would his career be in jeopardy if he allowed himself to have any sort of relationship with her?

The day ended as it had begun for Pippa, with her feeling miserable and alone.

Surprisingly she slept, but her dreams were wild, fantasy dreams where someone was making love to her. She wanted it to be Richard, but his face was in darkness and she could never see who it was. Then, just when it seemed as if she would find out the identity of her mystery lover, the scene shifted and she was in Casualty assisting with an RTA. It was a young boy who had been brought in, and Pippa was struggling to take his crash helmet off. His face was covered in blood, and when she finally wrested the helmet away she recoiled in horror to find that the face on the pillow was Richard's.

She awoke terrified and shaking. It was still dark, and she lay for several moments with her heart racing, trying to convince herself that it had only been a dream.

She turned over to try to see her clock, then she remembered it was Boxing Day and she was off duty. Other memories crowded in, and with a groan she buried her face in the pillow as she remembered that Richard wasn't interested in her and that he would probably be going away.

Pippa couldn't ever remember feeling this way about anyone before; there had, of course, been times when she had fancied herself in love, but never before had she experienced this intensity of feeling for anyone, and her response to that one kiss had left her shaken and disbelieving. For her emotions to have been so completely reversed, to have gone from actually disliking this man to this wild intensity of longing for him, made her begin to doubt her own sanity.

At last, when she could no longer make any sense of her shattered feelings, she climbed out of bed and filled the kettle to make some tea, then padded to the shower-room.

It was a loud and persistent knocking on her door that finally brought her back to reality. Pulling on her towelling bathrobe, she opened the door a few inches and peered out.

Richard stood on the landing.

She opened the door wider and stared at him in amazement.

'Philippa, I've just had a call from the hospital.' His voice was low and urgent. 'There's a red alert; they're calling in all off-duty staff.'

'Give me two minutes,' she said.

While he waited she threw on a tracksuit, knowing she had a uniform at the hospital to change into, then, pausing only to collect her bag, coat and keys, she joined him.

As they left the house he indicated her car on the forecourt. 'Shall we go in your car? It'll be quicker than getting the bike from the garage.'

'Of course,' she said, unlocking the door and praying that this time the car wouldn't let her down.

It started first time, and it wasn't until they pulled out on to the main road that she realised that the gentle mist of the night before had turned to a thicker fog. It took all her concentration to drive, and they remained silent until they were actually approaching the hospital, then Pippa said, 'Do you know the nature of the alert?'

'A motorway crash,' Richard replied briefly, then added, 'Hardly surprising in this fog.'

There was no time to speculate on the strangeness of the situation, that Richard should be sitting beside her in her car after her night of emotional turmoil; all that concerned her at that moment was that lives were in danger and their professional expertise was required.

They heard the klaxons before they entered the grounds as one ambulance after another swung through the gates escorted by police cars and motorbikes.

'Good God!' muttered Richard as for a moment they sat in the car park watching as if transfixed, then something galvanised him into action and he said, 'Right, let's go.'

They ran across the car park, joined as they went by other running figures as more and more members of staff answered Casualty's cry for help.

As they hurried into the unit the look of relief on Derek Henderson's face as he caught sight of Richard was only too obvious.

'Thank God you're here,' he muttered. 'Fortescue's in charge, but, to put it bluntly, he simply hasn't got your organising ability.'

'What have we got, Derek?' asked Richard as he struggled into his white coat.

'A coach full of pensioners on a trip to a pantomime,' explained the charge nurse. 'Apparently it hit the central reservation, collided with a minibus coming the other way, then, in the fog, other traffic piled into the back of the wreckage. So far we have multiple fatalities and dozens of serious injuries. Red alert operation is under way.' He glanced up and saw Pippa. 'Thanks for coming in, Pippa,' he said. 'Go and report to Sister Gould; we need all the help we can get.'

Pippa changed into her uniform in record time,

then reported to Rose Gould, who was in the administration area directing staff as they arrived to areas where they were most needed.

'Oh, good, Pippa,' she said. 'We need every pair of hands, but it's good to have members of our own team who know the ropes. Now, I want you to go down to the red alert area first—you'll find Nurse Sanders down there, and two porters. Help them to bring up the emergency supplies. After that I want you over in Accident and Emergency. Don't worry,' she added as she saw Pippa's expression, 'you'll be fine. They'll tell you what to do.'

As Pippa went off to the red alert area which Julie had previously shown her she felt a sudden warm glow, for it was the first time since she'd been on Casualty that she had really been made to feel one of the team.

She worked tirelessly to help to carry the emergency supplies up to Casualty, finding reserves of strength she never knew she had, then when they had finished she hurried to A and E.

She was unprepared, however, for the sight which met her eyes as one ambulance after another arrived bearing patients with quite horrific injuries.

The ambulance crews had already radioed in to explain the nature of the injuries of the patients they were carrying, so the team that met each vehicle had some idea which category patient they were dealing with.

At first sight it looked a muddle, but Pippa quickly realised that everything was under control and, depending on the severity of their condition,

patients were being allocated either to cubicles,
one of the treatment-rooms or the resuscitation
area.

Derek directed her to one of the treatment-
rooms, where she found the team in charge working over two patients. Richard was one of the
doctors, together with Dr Patel, his locum, and
they were assisted by Julie Acland and two other
nurses whom Pippa hadn't seen before.

Pippa saw that one of the patients was an elderly
lady who had obviously been neatly dressed in a
tweed skirt and twin-set for her trip to the pantomime, but these had now been cut away to reveal
her injuries. A twisted piece of metal had become
embedded in her side and the team were preparing
her for emergency surgery to be carried out by Mr
Fortescue.

As Julie caught sight of Pippa she indicated for
her to assist with setting up an intravenous infu-
sion, as the woman had lost a great deal of blood.

From that moment on Pippa became caught up
in a gruelling and relentless round of blood-press-
ure checks, erecting saline drips, applying pressure to open wounds, administering oxygen,
helping to treat shock, and talking to and reassuring one patient after another.

Some of the more serious injuries were quite
appalling, like the child who had been flung
through the windscreen of a car or the man who
had got out of his car to try to help and had been
run over by two other vehicles in the fog. He was
still alive, but would lose both his legs.

Some victims had sustained severe head injuries, and as Pippa worked mechanically, fetching

and carrying and doing as she was told, she seemed to find some mechanism that shut down her emotions and allowed her to deal with whatever arrived without becoming emotionally involved.

Afterwards she was to wonder whether, if she had known what she was going to witness, she would have been able to cope. As it was, she had no time to think, she quite simply got on with the job.

Once Mr Fortescue sent her to X-Ray for some urgent films, and as she entered Reception the scene that met her eyes was unbelievable. She had never seen so many people packed into one space. Some were walking wounded who were waiting for staff to attend to their injuries, others were waiting to collect patients, and yet others had arrived after hearing of the accident on the radio or the television and were desperate for news of relatives or friends.

The police were much in evidence, helping the hard-pressed medical staff, as were the hospital chaplain, social workers and two priests who had come in from town.

As the day wore on Pippa found that she too, when she wasn't assisting with the injured, was called upon to comfort distraught, bereaved relatives.

The more seriously injured had been some of the first to arrive at the hospital, then had followed a lull as the walking wounded were brought in, mostly passengers who had been sitting in the rear of the coach and had been hit by broken glass.

Much later had come more very seriously

injured who had had to be cut from the wreckage by the fire service. Some of these were dead on arrival and were taken directly to the already crowded mortuary to await identification and post-mortems.

It was quite late in the day, when Derek ordered her to go to the staff-room, that Pippa became aware of her own body's needs and she realised she hadn't had anything to eat or drink all day.

In Reception she passed Richard, and in spite of the turmoil her heart ached at the sudden sight of him. To her surprise, instead of merely passing by he paused and touched her arm.

'Are you all right?' he asked gently.

'Yes, I'm fine. Derek's just banished me to the staff-room.'

'Good. Get some rest, I'm afraid it isn't over yet.'

'Are they still bringing people in?'

'I think they've just brought in the last, but we've no more room. The wards are full; we'll have to transfer some patients.'

Pippa was struck by the fatigue in his eyes.

'Have you had a break, Richard?' she asked softly.

He smiled and his eyes met hers. 'Don't worry about me. . . I'm used to it, but it's all new to you.'

She was surprised and touched by his apparent concern for her, and as their gaze held for a moment it was as if the chaos around them had ceased and they were quite alone.

A sudden shout from one of the cubicles broke the spell.

'Dr Lawton. . .quickly. . .we have a patient bleeding heavily!'

'I'll be right there,' he called, then with a nod to Pippa he was gone.

She watched as he disappeared inside the cubicle and whisked the curtains shut behind him, then with a sigh she walked away from the madness, down the corridor to the rest-room.

The remainder of the day passed in a blur, and afterwards Pippa found she could only recall isolated incidents, images that became etched in her mind for all time; the tough skinhead sobbing helplessly when told his grandmother had died in the coach, the Roman Catholic priest sitting in the waiting-room giving a tiny baby its bottle of milk, and the moment when a distraught father's fear turned to joy when he found that his twin daughters, who had been passengers in the minibus, were both unharmed.

It was late evening before Casualty finally began to clear, the remaining patients unable to be accommodated by Whitford being transferred by ambulance or helicopter to other hospitals outside the area.

The original team who had started the day had insisted on remaining until things were more or less back to normal, but there was of course a backlog of ordinary Casualty patients for the night staff to contend with.

When it was finally time to go off duty, Pippa was thanked by both Sister Gould and Derek Henderson for the part she had played. As she zipped up her anorak over her old tracksuit she looked round for Richard, then she realised he was in the office talking to Mr Fortescue.

Slowly she ambled out of the unit to the car park, taking in great lungfuls of cold night air as she went. She hadn't realised just how exhausted she was until she got into her car and relaxed for the first time that day.

She didn't know how long she waited for Richard, because eventually she must have dozed off. The next thing she was aware of was someone tapping on the car window. With a start she opened her eyes and wondered where she was. The windows had become steamed up, and automatically she wound down the driver's window.

'Whatever are you still doing here?' demanded Richard. 'Derek said he'd sent you home hours ago.'

'I was waiting for you.'

'For me? But why?'

'Well, I didn't think you'd be able to get home.'

He stared at her, then his expressioin softened and he said, 'I could have got hospital transport to run me home.'

'Oh, I never thought of that. I just thought you'd be stranded without the bike.'

He opened the car door. 'Move over,' he said. 'I'll drive you home—you must be exhausted.'

'Yes, I suppose I am really.' Pippa yawned and moved awkwardly across to the passenger-seat, while he climbed in beside her. 'What time is it?'

'It's after twelve. I got caught up with old Fortescue, he wanted to go over everything again. Mind you, I've got to hand it to him, he did a brilliant job today.'

He drove out of the hospital entrance, raising his hand to the night porter on duty in the lodge as they passed, while Pippa snuggled drowsily down in her seat. She was more than content to let Richard drive, and as they sped through the empty streets she allowed herself the luxury of watching him, of drinking in every detail of his profile as if she could store it and take it out and relive the memory if he went away.

The thought of him going was almost more than she could bear, and on that particular night, in her state of exhaustion, it was certainly more than her brain could cope with.

When they reached Maple House and quietly let themselves in she was surprised to find that as they climbed the stairs his hand was firmly beneath her elbow.

When they reached the landing, for a brief moment she allowed herself to lean against him. Then, just when she thought he would leave her and disappear into his flat as he had the night before, he indicated for her to unlock her door.

He followed her inside, and as she took off her anorak he moved to the kitchen and filled the kettle. Content to let him take over, she sank down on to the sofa and, fighting waves of tiredness, rested her head on the back and closed her eyes.

It was the touch of his hand on hers that brought her back to reality and he handed her a mug of hot, sweet tea.

She smiled sleepily up at him. 'Did you think I might be suffering from shock?' she joked.

'You may well be, after the sights you've seen today,' he said as he sat down beside her.

'It was pretty awful, wasn't it?' she said weakly, then, realising that her hands had started to shake, she set her mug down on the table.

'You're not on duty tomorrow, are you?' Richard asked.

She shook her head. 'Are you?' Even as she asked the question she remembered. 'Oh, no, of course you're not, you're going to Edinburgh. . .' Her voice cracked and she trailed off miserably.

He nodded. 'Yes, I'm away first thing in the morning.' He was watching her closely as he spoke, then setting down his own mug he lifted one of her hands. 'What is it, Philippa?' he asked quietly. 'What's wrong?'

'I don't want you to go away.' There, she'd said it. Admitted it, not only to herself but to him as well.

Slowly he reached out and with his other hand he touched her cheek, gently drawing her face round to his. 'Why don't you want me to go?' His voice was husky now.

Pippa shrugged and gulped. 'I don't know. . .' Miserably she shook her head, then helplessly she looked up and into his grey eyes. 'I suppose I must be in love with you,' she blurted out at last. They stared at each other for an indefinable period of time, then with a deep sigh Richard lowered his head.

'I thought you might say that,' he said at last, and there was an unmistakable note of defeat in his voice.

'Well, is it so terrible? I couldn't help it, I certainly didn't want it to happen. Why, at the beginning I didn't even like you and I don't think you particularly liked me, and I certainly don't expect you to feel the same way now.' She choked slightly after her outburst, and, to her humiliation, sudden angry tears sprang to her eyes. Then she became aware that Richard's fingers had tightened over her own and she threw him a half-fearful glance, wondering what his reaction would be.

'Oh, Philippa!' He sighed, and she was struck by the lines of tiredness around his eyes. 'If only you knew!'

'If only I knew what?' She looked bewildered, but he had fallen silent again, almost as if he was afraid of saying too much.

'It could never be, you know. . .you and I,' he said at last, and, startled, Pippa looked up. 'For a start, I'm much older than you—it just wouldn't be fair, you're still a student, you want fun in your life, fun and young friends, while I. . .well I'm a different type. My work is my driving force, or at least I thought it was. . .'

'Don't you think my work is important to me?' she interrupted, and when he didn't reply she said, 'Falling in love wasn't exactly on my agenda either, you know. I have my finals to take yet, and qualifying was the most important thing in my life.'

'Was?' Richard asked softly.

'Yes—was,' she said almost angrily. 'Now, I don't even know what is.'

'I think,' he said slowly, 'it will be for the best all round if I do go to Edinburgh.'

She sighed, and in a gesture of defeat combined with mind-numbing tiredness she rested her head against his shoulder.

He slid his arm around her, drawing her closer to him and resting his face against her hair.

She hadn't meant to sleep, in fact at first she'd tried to fight her weariness in an effort to savour every precious moment spent with him, but, in the end, she had had to give in, and she had fallen asleep in his arms.

Yet again, her dreams were of Richard, but this time there was nothing horrific about them. This time she dreamt he really was making love to her, possessing her with his hands and his lips, arousing her to heights she had never believed possible, her body throbbing with an alien desire, then overwhelmed by an infinite sweetness that flooded her senses, leaving her at peace.

When she awoke it was morning, and Richard had gone. She was still wearing her tracksuit, but he must have lifted her on to a chair while he pulled out the sofa-bed, then laid her on the bed and covered her with her duvet.

For a long time she lay staring up at the ceiling, thinking about what had happened. How she had confessed her feelings to Richard, how he had told her nothing could ever work between them, that there were too many differences, and how finally he had said it would be better for them both if he did go to Edinburgh to work. And it wasn't until then that it occurred to her that he still hadn't spoken of his own feelings. She was no nearer knowing whether he had actually felt anything for her or whether she had imagined the passion that had flared between them. And if he went away she probably never would know, she thought with a sigh as she climbed out of bed, the fantasy of her dream dissolving with the lightening of the sky.

CHAPTER TWELVE

PIPPA spent the morning cleaning her flat, finding the physical work therapeutic in her present frame of mind, then just before lunch her doorbell rang, indicating there was someone to see her at the main entrance to Maple House.

When she opened the front door she found Claire on the step.

'Claire! Come in,' she invited. 'Am I glad to see you! How was Christmas?'

'Not as bad as I'd thought,' replied Claire, stepping into the hall.

Pippa would have closed the door behind her, but a sudden shout from the drive made both girls turn. Tim Barnes was trundling up the drive, a holdall in one hand and a rucksack on his back.

'Wherever's he been? The Alps?' Claire laughed as they waited for him.

'Would you believe, home for two days over Christmas?' smiled Pippa. 'Apparently his mother always stocks him up with goodies when he comes back.'

'Had a good time, girls?' Tim dumped his holdall on to the hall floor and eased off his rucksack with a groan. 'Lord, that's heavy! Have you missed me?' He looked from one to the other of them.

'I've been home,' replied Claire. 'But Pippa might have noticed you weren't around.'

'Well, my love? Has absence made the heart

grow fonder?' Tim turned to Pippa, giving her a quick kiss on the cheek.

'Sorry, Tim, I hardly had time to notice you were gone,' she told him.

'Will you listen to her?' He threw a despairing glance at Claire. 'Here I am, eating my heart out over the girl, and she says she hasn't even noticed that I haven't been around! Too busy living it up, I suppose?'

'Not exactly,' said Pippa quietly. 'We had a red alert yesterday.'

'What!' exclaimed Claire and Tim simultaneously.

'You are joking?' Tim's eyes narrowed.

Pippa shook her head. 'No, it's perfectly true. It was a coach smash on the motorway in the fog. Didn't you see it on the news?'

They both shook their heads, and Claire said, 'We didn't switch the telly on all over Christmas.'

'Neither did we.' Tim shook his head in disbelief. 'I don't know—I turn my back for five minutes and it all happens. There's never any excitement when I'm around.'

'I could have done without that sort of excitement on a Boxing Day,' said Pippa, then added, 'Or any day, come to that.'

'Was it pretty grim?' asked Claire, suddenly concerned.

'You could say that, yes,' agreed Pippa, then, as they both appeared to be waiting for her to elaborate, she said, 'There were sixteen killed and dozens injured. They were bringing people in all day. Some had to be cut from the wreckage——'

'Wasn't it your day off?' interrupted Tim.

Pippa nodded. 'Yes, but all off-duty staff were called in. They bleeped Dr Lawton and he came and called me. We ended up doing a double shift. There just weren't enough staff available. . .' She trailed off, then glanced round. 'Are we going to stand here all day? Come on, Claire, come up to the flat and have some lunch—you're on duty at one, aren't you?'

Claire nodded. She seemed dumbstruck by what she had just heard, and in silence she followed Pippa upstairs while a somewhat subdued Tim disappeared to his own flat.

Over lunch Pippa brought the subject round to Claire's personal problems.

'I had several long talks with my father,' said Claire thoughtfully in answer to Pippa's question.

'And what did he say about your training?' prompted Pippa.

'Just what you thought he'd say.' Claire sighed and stared out of the window at the bare branches of the trees in the avenue below. 'You were quite right, Pippa. There was no way he would have wanted me to give up my nursing and go home.' She paused reflectively. 'Of course he's desperately lonely, but he does now seem to be getting a grip on things again.'

'Is there no chance of your mother going back?' asked Pippa quietly.

Claire sighed and shook her head. 'No, I think the rift is too wide now.'

'And what about your brothers? Has your father made any arrangements regarding them?'

Claire smiled and visibly seemed to cheer up. 'That's the one bright spot on the horizon, as far as I can see. My grandmother's moving in for the time being. Dad's going to get someone to help with the shopping and the housework, but Granny's going to do the cooking, and she'll at least be there for the boys.'

'I'm so glad, Claire, I really am,' said Pippa. 'I don't think I could have stood it if you'd gone away.'

Claire put her elbows on the table and stared searchingly at her friend. 'Right, that's quite enough about me. Now I want to hear about you.'

'Me? What about me?' Pippa gave a weak smile, but she knew she couldn't fool her friend any longer.

'I'm sorry, Pippa, but I've got to say it—you look absolutely dreadful! I noticed it as soon as you opened the door.'

Pippa shrugged. 'I told you, we had one hell of a day yesterday. . .a double shift. I'm shattered, that's all.'

'No, Pippa, that's not all,' said Claire firmly. 'There was something wrong before I went away. I want to know what it is.'

As Pippa fought for the right words, Claire leaned across the table and took hold of her hands. 'Pippa,' she said urgently, 'look at me—that's right. Now, tell me, is it Richard Lawton?' She stared at her friend for a long moment, then she dropped her hands. 'OK, you don't have to tell me, it's written all over your face. So what's happened?'

Helplessly Pippa shook her head and swallowed, fighting the tears that seemed only too ready to spring to her eyes. 'That's just it,' she whispered at last. 'Nothing has happened, neither is it likely to.'

'What do you mean?' Claire frowned.

'It looks as if he's going away. He has an interview for a job in Edinburgh today.'

'An interview? Well, that doesn't necessarily mean he'll get the job.'

Pippa shrugged. 'Even if he doesn't, I'm not sure that will change anything.'

'What do you mean? Does he know how you feel about him?'

Pippa nodded miserably.

'And how does he feel about you?'

'That's the whole point. I'm not sure. . .but I'm pretty certain he doesn't feel the same. Let's face it, if he did, he wouldn't want to go away, would he?'

Still frowning, Claire stood up. 'Let's get this straight. . .hasn't he given any indication at all how he feels about you?'

Pippa sighed and looped her long hair behind her ears. 'Well, at one point I thought he really did feel something, then later he told me there couldn't be anything between us because I was too young and still a student. He also hinted that his career comes first and that he doesn't have time for a serious relationship.'

'Well, let's face it, Pippa, you've felt that way yourself until now.' Claire threw her a sharp glance, and must have seen the misery on her face, because she added, 'But this time it's serious, isn't it?'

'Yes, Claire, it's serious. I've never felt like this

before about anyone—you do understand what I mean, don't you?'

'Oh, yes, I understand,' replied Claire. 'I feel the same about Tony. I never meant anything to happen there—but it has, I just couldn't stop it. Has anything happened yet? You know what I mean, have you. . .?'

Pippa shook her head quickly. 'No, nothing like that.'

Claire stared at her helplessly, then she sighed. 'Maybe he just isn't into romance and relationships and that sort of thing. Do you remember at the beginning how much you detested him? You don't think it could just be a bad case of infatuation? You know, attraction for a highly unsuitable older man?'

Pippa shook her head. 'I really don't know what to think, Claire. My mind is just going round and round in circles.'

Suddenly Claire glanced up at Pippa's clock.

'Oh, my goodness, is that the time? I must fly— I'll be late, and Sister will slaughter me, especially after my being on leave over Christmas.'

Pippa stood up. 'I'll give you a lift to the hospital,' she said, reaching for her car keys.

'Oh, that's all right. I'll probably be able to get a bus—besides, you don't want to go to the hospital on your day off.'

'It's OK, I was going to go for a drive anyway. I thought I'd go over to Long Acre. I've got some serious thinking to do.' Pulling a face, Pippa followed her friend from the flat.

* * *

It was a crisp sunny day after the fog of the day before, and after Pippa had dropped Claire off at the hospital she drove slowly over to Long Acre, a local woodland area of great natural beauty by the river.

During the summer months the area would have been packed with tourists, but now, in winter, in spite of the brightness of the day, it was deserted.

Pippa drove the car beneath a cluster of beech trees on a point overlooking the river and switched off the engine.

The calm and tranquillity of the scene before her was in marked contrast to the drama of the previous day, and as she stared out across the calm water to a belt of deep green pines on the far bank Pippa found herself thinking for a moment of those who had lost their lives or a loved one in the horror.

She knew the incident had affected her deeply and that it was something she would remember for the rest of her life. She also knew that, coming as it had at a time of personal trauma in her own life, the memory would carry a note of extra poignancy.

With a sigh she opened the door and stepped out on to a bed of thick russet leaves, then, locking the car, she made her way between the tall smooth trunks to the river's edge.

She was warmly clad in a thick cream sweater, jeans and a dark green quilted body-warmer, so she hardly noticed the chill in the air as she stood on the river bank. Directly below her was a partly submerged log, and around it the water flowed faster in little eddies. She watched for a long time, and the water seemed to have a calming effect on her jangled nerves as gradually she came to the conclusion that she would just have to try and get Richard out of her mind.

It had seemed unbearable when she had first heard that he might be going away, but now she wondered if perhaps he had been right and it was for the best. Maybe if he was no longer around, if she didn't have to see him, watch him at work or meet him on the stairs at Maple House, she might slowly start to get over having loved him.

It was the sound of a sudden gunshot further along the river bank that broke into her thoughts. It was immediately followed by the loud cawing of a flurry of rooks rising protestingly into the sky around the tops of a group of tall leafless trees.

Pippa lifted her head and listened. The shot wasn't repeated, but it was then that she heard the sound of an approaching motorbike.

She couldn't see the road from where she was standing, but as the sound of the engine changed she realised the rider had turned off the road and was coming through the trees to the parking spot under the beeches.

Her heart began to beat very fast. Her first thought, that it might be Richard, dismissed when she remembered he was in Edinburgh, was replaced by a twinge of fear when she realised she was in a very vulnerable position, alone on the riverbank.

The sound of the engine ceased, and in the silence that followed Pippa cautiously lifted her head. The rider was still hidden from her view by the trees and she heard, rather than saw, his approach as he tramped through the thick carpet of dead leaves.

As he came into her line of vision her heart seemed to turn over. Dressed in his black leathers, he had taken off his crash helmet and his dark hair was ruffled as if he had run his fingers through it.

When he saw her he stopped, and for a long moment they simply stared at each other.

In the end it was Pippa who broke the silence. 'I thought you were in Edinburgh,' she said.

'I didn't go,' he replied simply, and her heart flipped crazily again.

'You didn't. . .?'

He shook his head. 'No. I telephoned and cancelled the interview.'

'Does that mean you've decided to take Mr Fortescue's job at Whitford?' She held her breath as she waited for his reply.

'It does. I've been to the hospital this morning to tell them my decision. I saw your friend Claire while I was there. She seemed very surprised to see me. Apparently you'd only just told her I was in Edinburgh.'

'How did you know where I was?'

'Claire told me that as well, so I came to find you. Philippa, we need to talk,' he said.

'Do we? I thought we'd said all there was to say.'

Richard moved towards her then, and, taking her arm, he said, 'Let's walk.'

They walked slowly along the riverbank, and for a time there was an awkward silence between them. Pippa hardly dared to hope that his decision not to go to Edinburgh might have anything to do with her. She threw him a curious glance and saw that a frown creased his forehead while a pulse throbbed at the corner of his jaw.

Suddenly she could bear it no longer; she had to know.

'Why have you decided not to go to Edinburgh?' she asked. 'You seemed so determined last night.'

'I've done a lot of thinking,' he explained.

'Really? Am I allowed to know what conclusion you've come to?' Pippa raised her eyebrows questioningly, almost teasingly, but he remained deadly serious.

'I can't go to Edinburgh because I can't bear to leave you.' He stated it firmly but quietly.

She stopped and stared at him, unable to believe her ears. Hadn't it only been the night before, when she had told him that she didn't want him to go because she was in love with him, that he'd told her it could never work out between them?

He must have read her thoughts, because he too stopped and, taking her hands, he stared down at her.

'But. . .' she looked bewildered '. . .last night you said. . .you said——'

With one hand he covered her lips, stifling her protests. 'I know what I said, every excuse I made, but I was deluding myself if I thought I could carry on with my life as if I'd never met you.'

'You said I was too young for you. I thought. . .'

'I know, and that still bothers me, but it doesn't alter how I feel. Honestly, Philippa, I've had to fight my feelings for you almost from the moment I met you. I was instantly attracted to you.'

'But I thought you didn't like me.'

'I suppose in my efforts to deny my feelings I must have given that impression, but I just can't explain what you've done to me. I found I could talk to you, I've told you things I could never before bring myself to talk about, and I can't fight how I feel any longer. . .' With a low groan he pulled her into his arms, and just before his mouth covered hers he murmured fiercely, 'I love you, Philippa, and I want you.'

She felt a thrill pierce her body as she happily surrendered to the urgency of his kiss, while his hands roamed demandingly, possessively over her body, evoking sensations deep inside that touched a chord somewhere in her memory.

It was another distant gunshot, followed by the inevitable cawing of the rooks, that finally interrupted them, and with a sigh Richard lifted his head.

Almost faint with the overwhelming knowledge that he loved her, Pippa gazed up at him, loving every detail of his face, the straight nose and grey eyes, the firm line of his jaw and the dark hair that fell forward over his brow.

At last he looked down at her, smiling when he saw her look of open adoration. 'This was the last thing I intended to happen. I was so involved in my work that I never even considered the possibility of falling in love.'

'But what about your career?' Pippa suddenly looked anxious. She knew how much it meant to him, and she didn't want to stand in his way.

'My career is still very important to me and it always will be, but other people cope, and there has to be a way round things.'

'But Edinburgh was important, wasn't it?'

He shrugged. 'Yes, I suppose it was, but only up to a point. I dare say I shall get on just as well at Whitford. But talking of careers, there's yours to consider as well.'

Pippa frowned. 'There's no problem there. I shall finish my training and I hope I'll qualify— that's if I can concentrate, of course!' She looked up at him and noticed the pulse throbbing again at the corner of his jaw. 'What's the matter, Richard? Are you worried there may be talk about our relationship?'

He nodded grimly. 'I've never before worried about what people think, but now I'm concerned about the fact that you're still a student. I don't want any malicious talk about you.' He sighed, and, slipping his arm around her, turned and walked with her away from the river beneath the branches of the tall beeches.

'I even considered going to Edinburgh and then asking you to join me there after your finals. . .' he began.

'And. . .?' She looked up enquiringly.

'I knew I couldn't bear being away from you, even for a year. So I came to the conclusion that I have to stay here, at least until you've done your finals. . .after that, who knows?' Then, tightening his grip on her, he said, 'Philippa, I've rambled on, probably said far more than I should, but I have to know, were you serious last night when you said you were in love with me?'

'Oh, Richard!' She laughed. 'Of course I was. I was never more serious about anything in my life. I was devastated when I thought you were going away, and I really thought you didn't care about me at all.'

Roughly he pulled her close again, staring deeply into her eyes before covering her lips with his. Between kisses he said, 'Oh, God, if only you knew! All those times in Casualty when I had to fight a tremendous urge to make violent love to you on one of the treatment couches!'

'Can you imagine what Sister Gould would have made of that?' Pippa chuckled.

'She'd probably have turned a blind eye and let us get on with it—salt of the earth, is our Rose. But it's not Rose I'm concerned about, it's your tutor and my consultant.'

'Do you think they'll be much trouble when they find out?' asked Pippa.

'Only recently they caught a houseman in bed with a first-year student and there was one hell of a stink—in fact it was me who had to reprimand the doctor!'

'Well, it's not as if we've done anything like that!' exclaimed Pippa indignantly.

Richard was silent, and when he didn't reply she glanced up at him. There was a curious expression on his handsome face.

'As it happens, Nurse Ward,' he said solemnly, 'I'm afraid we have.'

'Have what?'

'Spent the night in bed together.'

She stared at him, her eyes opening wide as the implication of what he was saying suddenly hit her and she recalled again the memory of a deep desire that had not seemed unfamiliar when he had kissed her only a few moments ago.

'Richard. . .just how long were you in my room last night?' she asked at last.

He lowered his head so that she couldn't see the expression in his eyes.

'Philippa, I'm sorry, but I'm afraid I have to confess I was there all night.'

'What!' She gazed at him, stupefied. She knew that in her state of exhaustion he must have put her to bed, but she had imagined that he had then gone straight to his flat. Could it be that what she had thought had been a dream had actually happened? 'You mean you. . .?'

He nodded, but he had the grace to look shamefaced. 'Yes, after I'd put you into bed I stayed. I believe it was then, watching you sleep, that I realised just how much you've come to mean to me. You looked so lovely with your hair spread all over the pillow.'

At his words Pippa felt the colour tinge her cheeks and she lowered her head in sudden embarrassment, still uncertain exactly what had happened.

But Richard didn't seem to notice. 'Later I fell asleep beside you—I guess I was as tired as you were.'

'So when did you leave?'

'About six o'clock, I think. You were still sound asleep. The trouble is, I can't be certain that no one saw me leave, and you know what the hospital grapevine is like.'

Pippa frowned, then threw him a sharp glance, uncertain whether he was being serious or not.

'You know, Philippa,' he gave an exaggerated sigh, 'there's only one thing for it. I'll just have to make an honest woman of you, and that will stop all the wagging tongues and even your tutor won't be able to complain.'

Then, with a sudden deep chuckle, he caught her face between his hands, entangling them once again in the wild cloud of her hair. 'You will marry me, won't you?' he said urgently.

'Of course I will.' She said it instantly, unhesitatingly, irrespective of the fact that only a month ago it would have been the last thing she would have imagined agreeing to. But a month ago she hadn't met Richard Lawton, and since then nothing had been quite the same.

Much later, when he reluctantly pulled away from her, he said, 'I heard this morning that my new apartment is almost ready, but first I'd like you to come and see if you like it. If you do perhaps you'd like to choose the décor. Your flat always seems so warm and cosy.'

'It's strange, you know,' said Pippa as they began to walk back through the dead leaves, 'but I moved to that flat at Maple House so I wouldn't have to share with anyone again, and here I am, just less than a month later, talking of moving out so that I can share your new apartment.'

'Ah, but this is different,' he said.

As they reached the parked vehicles he began to pull on his crash helmet, but as Pippa put her key in the lock, she paused.

'Richard?' she said curiously.

'Yes?' He lifted the helmet slightly so that he could hear her.

'Last night, in my flat. . .' she hesitated

'. . .when I was so tired. . .did anything happen. . .?'

His grey eyes widened. 'Ah, Philippa, my love, I too was pretty tired, so that's something we may never know.' He shook his head, then, raising his eyebrows questioningly before mounting his motorbike, he said, 'But I have an idea; why don't we go back there right now? And this time, I assure you, there'll be no problem; we'll both know what happens.'

Mills & Boon

Discover the thrill of 4 Exciting Medical Romances – FREE

FREE
BOOKS FOR YOU

In the exciting world of modern
medicine, the emotions of true love
have an added drama. Now you can
experience four of these
unforgettable romantic tales of passion
and heartbreak FREE – and look forward to
a regular supply of Mills & Boon
Medical Romances delivered direct to your door!

❧ ❧ ❧

Turn the page for details of 2 extra
free gifts, and how to apply.

An Irresistible Offer from Mills & Boon

Here's an offer from Mills & Boon to become a regular reader of Medical Romances. To welcome you, we'd like you to have four books, a cuddly teddy and a special MYSTERY GIFT, all absolutely free and without obligation.

Then, every month you could look forward to receiving 4 more **brand new** Medical Romances for £1.60 each, delivered direct to your door, post and packing free. Plus our newsletter featuring author news, competitions, special offers, and lots more.

This invitation comes with no strings attached. You can cancel or suspend your subscription at any time, and still keep your free books and gifts.

Its so easy. Send no money now. Simply fill in the coupon below and post it at once to -

Mills & Boon Reader Service, FREEPOST,
PO Box 236, Croydon, Surrey CR9 9EL

NO STAMP REQUIRED

✂ --

YES! Please rush me my 4 Free Medical Romances and 2 Free Gifts! Please also reserve me a Reader Service Subscription. If I decide to subscribe, I can look forward to receiving 4 brand new Medical Romances every month for just £6.40, delivered direct to my door. Post and packing is free, and there's a free Mills & Boon Newsletter. If I choose not to subscribe I shall write to you within 10 days - I can keep the books and gifts whatever I decide. I can cancel or suspend my subscription at any time. I am over 18.

EP20D

Name (Mr/Mrs/Ms) _____

Address _____

_____

_____ Postcode _____

Signature _____

mps
MAILING
PREFERENCE
SERVICE